HOW NOT TO BLEND

A LOVESTRONG STORY

SUSAN HAWKE

Cover Art Designed by Ana J Phoenix

Editing done by Courtney Bassett of LesCourt Author Services
Proofreading done by Lori Parks of LesCourt Author Services

https://www.lescourtauthorservices.com/

When you have a crush on your dad's best friend and there's nothing left to lose but your pride, you learn... How Not To Wait

Get your FREE copy of How Not To Wait
https://dl.bookfunnel.com/mx2r9719ru

Twitter:
https://twitter.com/SusanHawkeBooks

Facebook:
https://www.facebook.com/AuthorSusanHawke/

1

ANDY

"There's my pretty girl. How are you doing today, sweet cheeks?" I asked as I quickly moved to the doorway to offer an arm to help my grandmother to her chair. "Do you feel like a little somethin' somethin' for the tum-tum, or are we waiting for Helen to drag her lazy ass in here to feed you breakfast?" I didn't mind taking care of my gams, that's one of the biggest reasons I lived here. But her caregiver left a lot to be desired.

Gam-Gam looked like a queen as she peered up at me with a regal smile. The gaudy coral lipstick she wore was blinding against her pale skin as she patted my arm. "I won't say no to a cup of joe, especially if you wanted to be a doll and add in a splash of hooch for an old lady."

I snorted. "Sure thing. You go on and find me an old lady and I'll make that happen. But as for you? Sorry, sweetheart. It's a big ixnay on the ooch-hay after that double bypass you had this summer." Helping her into her chair, I tucked a pillow behind her back and kissed her cheek before wagging my finger in her face. "And quit trying to trick me, you little seductress. I'm not breaking those rules the hospital sent home with you."

"Oh, hush, princess. There's no need to go gettin' your panties in a bunch. You just tell me one thing—what the hell good is it to live a little bit longer if I don't get to damn well enjoy the life I'm living?" Gam-Gam arched a brow, crossing her arms over her chest as she glared up at me with a triumphant smile.

"Nice try, darlin'. Do us both a favor and save that shit for Helen, I'm immune to your pleas. I'm a hardhearted bitch when it comes to your health—so suck it up, buttercup." I giggled, stepping quickly out of range when she tried to swat my butt. "Now behave yourself and settle down. Here's the remote. Why don't you get started on your daily *Jerry Springer* marathon while I hook you up with some coffee and feed Satan? What is it with you and those shows anyway?"

Gams tittered. "Have you seen 'em? The people on that show are a mess. I bet if you met one of those Springer guests on the street they'd smell like a pungent blend of cheap perfume, weed, and cum. As soon as one of those crying girls starts declaring her undying love, I just know her honey's brother, cousin, or best friend is waiting in the wings to say they've been with her too." Gams shook her head while aiming the remote at the TV with a stiff-armed grip, biting her lip as if concentration were needed to make the magic stick work. Once she'd found her channel, she cranked up the volume and set the remote aside with a happy sigh before looking up at me again. "Are you still here? I thought you went to feed my baby boy. Best get going so you're not late today. And remember to be nice to your uncle while you're at it," Gam-Gam chastised as I headed for the kitchen. "My sweet baby is a blessing to us both."

I rolled my eyes at the word *uncle*. "I believe the word you meant to use was curse, or maybe even blight, but sure—we can go with blessing, if you prefer. Where is that little shit, anyway?" I looked around for the devil dog while I turned the Keurig on to warm. As soon as I walked over to his food bowl and shook the bag of kibble, the swinging doggy door that led to the back yard flipped up and the deceptively cute, black and toffee colored, fuzzy-faced, one-eyed pirate of a dog glared in at me, his crusty nose twitching for the scent of breakfast.

Okay, maybe he wasn't glaring. After all, surely resting bitch face was a given for a Pekinese who'd been born with one eye? He scampered in, following me over to the sink where I made quick work of mixing the dry kibble with a can of his fancy wet food to soften it. Devil dog pawed at my pant legs, growling up at me as if ordering me to hurry things along. "Patience, Beelzebub. It takes a few minutes to mix your daily kibble with the souls of the damned."

I fought back a laugh when the little fuzzball chuffed at

my comment. You could tell me till the cows came home that this dog didn't understand English, but moments like this begged to differ. As I bent to set his food down, he nipped at my wrist before plunging his flat little face into the bowl. "Haven't you ever heard that you shouldn't bite the hand that feeds you? Honestly, honey. You really need to learn some manners or grow opposable thumbs and feed your own damned self—just sayin'."

After giving his toffee-colored fur an unwanted scratch between the ears, I filled his water bowl before finally attending to the needs of the humans. The little stinkerbutt would be the first to tell you that was only as it should be.

"Did I hear you fussing at my baby boy?" Gam-Gam asked when I carried her coffee in a few minutes later, along with a small plate of buttered toast. "My poor angel has had a hard enough go of it, what with being born disabled. You need to have patience with him, Anderson."

"*Anderson?* Uh-oh, we're using the full name now? Dayumn... pull the claws back in, honey. Me and the devil dog have our own special relationship, you don't need to worry your pretty little head about it." I sat down in the chair beside her with my own cup of coffee, crossing an ankle over the opposite knee as I leaned back and pretended to relax while discreetly assessing her coloring and breathing.

Gam-Gam muted the TV and turned to me with a knowing smirk. "I'm not gonna keel over today, kiddo.

Drink your coffee and quit checking me out. If I wanted to feel a man's eyes on me, it wouldn't be from my own grandson—and he definitely wouldn't be gay, if you know what I mean."

The fluffy demon came running into the room as though he had a time schedule to keep, his tags jingling with each move. With one quick leap onto Gams' footstool and another to her lap, he settled himself in his place of honor and stared me down. Gam-Gams' hand immediately fell onto his back, running her fingers through his soft toffee-colored fur as the baby talk commenced. "There's my pretty boy. Who's my pretty boy? That's right, you are. Yes, you are, aren't you? Give mama some sugar, baby."

I had to look away while Gam-Gam let Satan put his black face right up to hers and lick her mouth. "Eww. Get a room, you two. It's way too early in the morning for that shit."

Gam-Gam giggled like a schoolgirl, smirking at me with smeared lipstick. "I have a room, lots of them—one of which I'm kind enough to let you live in, aren't I? Now you sit there and behave yourself before I make you lean over and let my baby give you kisses too. Hell, I probably should. Maybe a little sugar might sweeten you up a bit. Lord knows you aren't getting kisses anywhere else these days, or are you?" She arched her brow again, waiting expectantly for an answer. "You'd tell me if you were seeing any new gentleman callers, wouldn't you?"

I glanced at the clock and jumped up. "And there's my cue

to leave." Devil-dog bared his teeth when I reached out to scratch under his black, nearly nonexistent chin. He didn't growl, though; the little shit never did when Gam-Gam was in earshot. "You need anything before I head out the door, Gam-Gam?" I asked softly, all teasing put aside as I prepared to leave. "Did you take your heart medicine yet? You can't take that on an empty stomach; that's why I gave you the toast."

Gam-Gam rolled her eyes and shook her pillbox at me, a cagey look flashing in her eyes as she searched my face. "Quit worrying so much, you'll give yourself an ulcer. Or even worse, you'll get frown lines on your forehead. You know, people in our family do tend to wrinkle young. Hell, that's usually the precursor to the male pattern baldness that runs on my mother's side." She shrugged, waving a hand. "But I'm not telling you anything you don't already know, you've seen your father—the ass that he is."

"Wrinkles and premature baldness? Sweet, merciful mother Cher! You take that back, you harlot! Lies, I tell you! All lies! This is what happens when you hang out with the devil, you become a liar. Everyone knows Satan is the father of lies; I should've seen this coming." I gasped, crossing myself and sending a mental prayer up to any interested parties that she wasn't telling the truth about premature wrinkling. Although, now that she mentioned it, I did remember my father having an awful lot of wrinkles when I was a kid. And he was bald in his thirties, wasn't he? I was mentally calculating how old he would've been back then while I took my cup to the sink to rinse.

Deciding to worry about that another day, I grabbed my jacket from the coat hook on my way back through, slipping it on before I walked over to give Gam-Gam's cheek a kiss goodbye. She reached out and patted my hand where it rested on the arm of her chair as I bent. "You have a good day, princess. Maybe I'll have Helen put on a pot of stew this afternoon for our supper this evening, does that sound good?"

"That sounds fabulous," I said, licking my lips as I turned to leave. In a flash, Jeebus was off Gam-Gam's lap and chasing along beside me as I walked to the door. He was growling and nipping at my pant legs, but not loud enough for Gam-Gam to hear, of course. "Are you trying to tell me to have a nice day, Beelzebub?" I looked down at the little furball, crooning into his malevolent face as if he really were the sweetest little dog in the world. He lunged for my ankle as I slipped out the door, but I was faster.

"Not today, Satan!" I called through the door when I heard him pawing at the other side. "You gotta be faster than me if you want to chase me out the door." Despite our back and forth, I liked to think that the fuzzball and I actually had our own special relationship. Even if we didn't, I would put up with a lot more than that little guy could dish out just to see the smiles he put on Gam-Gam's face.

As I slipped into the driver's seat of my car, I pushed my concerns for Gam-Gam's health and any stray thoughts of the satanic canine aside. While the car warmed up, I went through my playlist and put on some soul-cleansing music for the drive to work. Today's selection came courtesy of the benevolent goddess Miss Britney herself, thank you very much. I sang along with my girl while I drove through town. Rockford Bluff wasn't much, but it had been an oasis when Gam-Gam had taken me in.

One of my favorite songs was ending right as I pulled up in front of the sprawling behemoth of a building that housed the town's small hospital on one side and dozens of the various, small-town medical practices we had to offer on the other. After a quick hair check in the visor mirror and a slow swipe of moisturizing gloss over my lips, I put my game face on and headed inside, ready to begin my day.

At seven forty-five in the morning, the lobby was already filled with people rushing off in different directions. The large, open area was all glass windows and doors—its vaulted ceiling soared up three floors, creating an atrium effect. Standing in this modern space, decorated only by benches, fake ficus trees, and the banks of elevators on either side of the space, one could almost forget they were living in a small town. Almost.

The coffee kiosk stood proudly at the back of the lobby, conveniently located between the elevators, yet too far from the flow of traffic to get in anyone's way. My coworker, Tracy, looked up with a bright smile as I breezed around the counter and stepped into our area.

"Good morning, sunshine. You're looking mighty chipper

today," I said, snagging an apron and slipping it over my head. "I take it the hot date went well last night?"

Tracy giggled, stepping away from the cups she'd been busily stacking and putting a well-manicured hand over her mouth as she blushed. "Oh, don't even get me started. I had the best time ever! It was so romantic, Andy. He even brought me flowers, can you believe it?"

I started prepping the espresso machine for the day while she talked. "He'd better have brought flowers, or I would've had to kick his sorry ass myself. That silly boy has been chasing after you for a month of Sundays. If he didn't put his best foot forward, I'd have called him a stupid idiot and been right to do it."

"It hasn't been that long," Tracy said defensively. "I was getting over a breakup; I wasn't going to just rush right into my next relationship. Michael understood that, so he gave me time before he made his move."

"Baby girl, if you call leaving you flirty love notes and accidentally running into you on purpose everywhere you went 'giving you time,' then we need to talk. Shit, he's lucky you didn't have his ass arrested for stalking. Besides, Michael hasn't just been trying to date you. That boy is courting you, honey." I turned to look at her, putting a hand on my hip as I shook my head. "Please tell me you at least followed my first date rules? At least six inches between you at all times and only a chaste kiss on the cheek at the door, right?"

I groaned at the guilty blush on her face. "*Girl*. Really? I give up. Basic dating rules dictate that you always leave them coming back for more. Take it from a true Southern belle, I wouldn't lead you wrong."

"Who says I didn't?" She winked and turned toward the counter as the first customer of the day approached. As soon as she saw who it was, Tracy turned back. "Dr. Hottie is early today. Should I make myself scarce while you get your flirt on?"

"Girl, please. You know it's not like that; now get out of here and fix his drink before you cramp my style," I hissed in a low voice, shooing her aside before turning with a welcoming smile to greet my crush.

Oh, yeah. Now this was how a man was meant to start his day. I resisted the urge to lick my lips as I feasted my eyes on the tall, dark-haired Adonis. He'd glance up long enough to hand me money every morning, those slate-gray eyes crinkling at the corners as he smiled politely. And what a smile. It was enough to even make a blind gal's heart go pitter-pat. As usual, he was too busy texting to make eye contact as he rattled off his regular order, leaving me free to drink in my fill of his fine self. "Large, triple-shot Americano with a dash of cinnamon, please."

"Here you go," Tracy said brightly, already handing me his drink before I even had him rung up. Our Dr. Hottie was as predictable as he was gorgeous. I held my breath and waited for the smile, trying not to swoon when it came in a flash. If I'd blinked, I'd have missed it. All too soon, he was dropping his change into the tip jar and rushing off toward the elevators that led to the medical practices with an absentminded thanks tossed over his shoulder.

I bit back a sigh when his fine ass stepped into a waiting car. As the doors closed, I watched him frowning at his screen and wondered if he'd ever notice me. And would I keel over on the spot if he did? Oh, well. At least I'd had my morning eye candy fix.

2

CORBIN

I was enjoying my lunch hour break between patients, eating a late lunch and going over a stack of charts, when my head nurse popped her head in my office door. "Dr. Davis? Sorry to bother you, hon, but you've got a call holding on line one. It's the school, sir. You probably ought to take it; they didn't sound like this was a social call."

"Is it ever? Thanks, Mandy." I groaned as I reached for the phone. "The joys of being a single parent to a teenager, am I right?"

"Don't I know it?" She laughed ruefully as she slipped back out of my office.

"This is Corbin Davis. How can I help you?" I spoke briskly as I answered the phone.

"Sorry to bother you, Doctor. This is Laura Blackwell. I'm the nurse over at Rockford High? I'm sorry to tell you this, but there was a bit of a scuffle in the gymnasium during fourth period. We'll need you to come pick your son Grayson up as soon as you can."

"A bit of a scuffle? Has my son been injured? I'm sorry, but I'm not understanding why I need to come pick him up over yet another schoolyard scuffle." I wrapped what was left of my sandwich in its napkin and tossed it in the wastebasket, my appetite effectively gone. "This is the third time in less than two months. What's going on over there at that school? Surely something can be done."

"We'd rather explain in person, Dr. Davis. It was more of a fight than a scuffle, to be perfectly honest. Grayson did sustain injuries, yes." She sounded almost apologetic as she lowered her voice, as though not wanting to be overheard by whoever else was in the office. "Unfortunately, we are taking action this time. In incidents like this, we're required to suspend all involved participants, no matter the cause. There's no way around it; you need to come down here, Doctor."

"Okay, tell him to sit tight and I'll be right there," I said quickly, ending the conversation and gritting my teeth as I fought the urge to slam the phone down as I hung it up. After taking a quick moment to lock the patient files in my desk drawer, I grabbed my keys and pocketed my cell before heading out to the reception area. "Mandy, can you either reschedule my afternoon patients or see if Hank can cover me? There's been an incident and I need to see to Grayson right now."

"Already on it, hon. You just go right on ahead and take care of Gray. I'll handle clearing your schedule." Mandy was already efficiently tapping her keyboard, her attention focused on the monitor.

"Thanks, you're a real peach, Mandy. I sure hope those bosses of yours appreciate you," I said with a grin as I backed toward the door.

Mandy's round face beamed with a cherubic yet maternal smile. "Oh, go on with you. Save that charm of yours for all those patients who pine over their beloved Dr. Dreamy."

I snorted at that one, waving a hand as I slipped out the door. My flirtatious patients were an ongoing office joke—a fact that was especially amusing to my staff, given the fact that most of my patients were senior citizens.

When I strode into the school office a short time later, I saw Grayson slouched in a chair across from the school secretary. He was still dressed in his gym clothes, staring sullenly at the floor with his arms crossed over his chest. I noted black smudges around both eyes, and a fair amount of swelling on the right one. My nostrils flared as I walked over to stand in front of him.

Grayson looked up at me with an insolent smirk. "What, they pulled you away from your precious patients? Sorry to intrude on your busy day, *Doctor Dad*."

I ignored the sarcasm and cut to the chase. "Save the sass, young man. What the hell is this shit about you fighting? I can't even begin to describe how disappointed I am right now. How many times do we need to have this discussion before you listen, Grayson? Neanderthals use fists, real men use their words." As I continued to lecture him, I didn't pay attention to who might be listening or hanging around. I was irritated when Gray didn't answer me and instead sat there stiffly, refusing to make eye contact.

"Excuse me, Dr. Davis." I turned to see a stern-looking older woman staring at me with pinched lips. "Perhaps you'd care to table your discussion for later? Your son needs immediate dental attention if he's to save his tooth." She held out a clear, plastic container with a tooth floating in blood-tinted water. "The tooth just fell out a few minutes before you arrived. I've spoken to the dentist's office you had listed on his file and they say there's a strong possibility that it can be saved if you get him there as soon as possible." She lowered her voice as she handed me the cup with a reproving glance. "It's a small window of time from what I understand, so you'll want to hurry."

I was stunned as I took the tooth and noted the dried blood around Gray's mouth for the first time. *Fuck me.* Welp, there goes my father of the year award. "Come on, Gray. Let's go," I said, turning for the door.

"Wait, you can't go just yet!" the secretary called out. "You'll need to sign the student out first, Dr. Davis."

Groaning internally, I fought the urge to roll my eyes as I wasted precious seconds by following their silly procedures. "How long is he to be suspended? I don't believe you told me that part," I said as I scrawled my name on the form.

"Five school days," the secretary said with a sniff, her eyes flitting over toward the chairs across from her. "We have a strict anti-bullying policy here at Rockford High. Both kids have been punished with the same amount of time; there are no shows of favoritism here."

As she said that, I glanced over my shoulder to see who she'd looked at and did a double take when I saw the big, football-player-looking sumbitch who'd been quietly sitting there the whole time. Clark Danvers. *Fan-fucking-tastic.* His father, Harold Danvers, was the ruling elder at our church and a thorn in my side thanks to the bigoted views he espoused in the name of God. Not only did my kid try to fight a linebacker, he had to go and pick the son of the biggest asshole I knew?

When I noticed the little shit smirking at Gray while he thought nobody was watching, it occurred to me that there was more going on here than I'd been told. I brushed the thought aside. Now wasn't the time to get into it, we had a tooth to save.

I motioned for Gray to follow as we headed for the car, already whipping my phone out to text my best friend Dana who worked at the dentist's office to see if Gray had an appointment already, and if so, what time they were expecting us.

Wincing when Gray slammed the door of my Jag, I let it

go. *Pick your battles, Corb.* I turned to say something to him, but he'd already slipped his earbuds in and was leaning back with his eyes firmly closed. When had my sweet little kid turned into this teenage asswipe? And how could I get my kid back? Was that even possible, or was I doomed to a lifetime of these moments? I bit back a sigh and pulled out of the lot. What a fucking day. I was ready for it to be over and it wasn't even two o'clock yet.

3
ANDY

"Hey, lookie there, honeybun. Isn't that Dr. Hottie?" Tracy nudged me in the side with her bony elbow, pointing toward the main entrance with her chin.

"Damn straight, I'd recognize the curve of that fine ass anywhere. Look at him go, would you? No, scratch that. I'm territorial about that view, so avert your eyes, hussy." Tracy rolled her eyes while I leaned around the edge of the cart to get a better view. "Damn, girl. That booty he's sporting is like a ripe peach that needs to be marked with my bite." I fanned my face and heaved a dreamy sigh as I watched said peach exit the premises. "I wonder where he's going in the middle of the day? I sure hope he didn't have an emergency or something."

"But just think... what if he did, and you were the only one who could help him through it? Like, what if his life depended on you being at his side to help battle whatever was troubling him? You could be the Robin to his Batman, tights and all. Are you man enough for the job, big guy?" Tracy pouted up at me playfully, accenting her words with a flutter of her lashes.

"You know I'd be on that like white on rice. All he'd have to do is call my name and I'd be there. Tights are optional, but you know me, I'm never against a classic accessory if it pulls a look together." I snickered and put two fingers in the center of Tracy's bratty forehead, nudging her back when she started making kissy faces and rude noises. "That's it, missy. You just wait until Romeo drops by to see you this afternoon. Payback's a bitch and so am I. Trust me on that one."

"Oooh," Tracy intoned with a shiver. "I'm *skeered* of you, drama queen. Whatever will you do, throw some glitter at me?"

"Don't tempt me, you know how much I like a bit of sparkle in my life." I waggled my eyebrows like an evil henchman, rubbing my hands together as though hatching my villainous plan.

This time Tracy did shiver. "Nope. Never mind. Just forget I even mentioned the word. Isn't glitter known as the herpes of the craft world because you literally can't ever get rid of it? And what is with that whole 'white on rice' thing anyway? Isn't rice inherently white? You Southerners have weird expressions." She chattered while cleaning the machine that was still a mess from our lunch rush while I got to work restocking the sugar packets.

"I don't know, something about when they started bleaching rice maybe? But can I just say that it's not Southern because it comes out of my mouth? It's just a saying... if you start questioning every old saying, then pretty soon you'll start to doubt whether your grandparents really walked five miles uphill through the snow in pouring rain to get to school every day when they were kids, and then society would start to crumble. Nobody needs that, sugar." I waved her off as I spoke absentmindedly, staring into space for a minute, already picturing the fabulous glitter bomb I could hide in her car. *Maybe if I wedged it between the seats...* I was startled back into the moment when a customer rapped on the counter with a loud knocking sound.

"Hellooo, are you two actually serving customers today or are you just standing there to hold up the counters and gossip?" *Oh, hayell no.* Before I could say a word in reply to the rude beeyotch standing in front of the register, Tracy pushed me back with a firm hand to the center of my chest as she turned to the woman with a perky smile.

"Forgive us, ma'am. What can we do for you today?" The woman huffed and gave her order to Tracy while I zipped my lip. *Sugar, Honey, Iced Tea.* Whoever had said the customer was always right had clearly never worked a service job.

The next several customers were just as rude. I'd always thought there was something about the midafternoon that brought the inner asshole out in people. I could never decide whether it was because the day wasn't moving fast enough, or if maybe they were just overgrown toddlers who needed a nap. I lifted a brow and pursed my lips when the current charmer said something that caught my attention.

I'd just placed his order on the counter when Prince Charming shot me a disgusted sneer. "Can I be frank? I'm curious as to whether that sparkly lip gloss you're wearing is within your company's approved dress code for male employees. I find it to be highly inappropriate for the workplace and I'm a bit surprised that your management allows it."

Tipping my weight onto one hip, I crossed my arms over my chest and waited for him to finish speaking while I counted back from ten. I held up a lightly closed fist, as if to examine my neatly manicured nails, while responding with a cool smile. "I don't know, hon. That's a right good question, now isn't it? I mean, *can* you be frank? It all depends on what your given name is, I suppose. If you really wanted to be Frank, and that's not your name, then you'd probably need to go to City Hall and pay a fee for a name change." I trailed off thoughtfully, ignoring the rest of his statement while I focused my brain power on the whole frank situation.

Tracy was suppressing a snicker, turning her back to the counter and busying herself with changing the garbage bag while I dealt with Prince Charming. His nostrils flared as he stared back at me. "Are you trying to be cute with me? Don't make me ask to see the manager."

"You know what, honey?" I laid on the Southern drawl as I spoke. "You're looking at the manager. But management isn't what you need. No. What you need is to meet sweet baby Jeebus, bless your heart. He'll put you to rights and let you know what's what, and that's just facts. Now as much as I'd *love* to continue this conversation about your given name, I really do need you to take your drink and move along because there are people waiting behind you. Y'all have a nice day now, you hear?"

I bit back a laugh as his complexion darkened into an interesting shade of magenta. "I'll be back to see your boss. There's bound to be someone on top of you. And don't think I won't mention you having brought religion into the workplace, either." I fluttered my fingers, ignoring his retort and resisting the urge to say that not every twink was a bottom.

Of course, I wasn't opposed to having someone top either. I liked to think that I was quite versatile like that. Instead of commenting, I cheerfully stuck to waving buh-bye as he stormed away. I was pleasantly surprised to find Dr. Hottie was the next in line, although I bit back my curiosity regarding the angry teen standing beside him.

"Back so soon? It's not tomorrow yet, is it? Because if it's time for your morning coffee, I surely must've forgotten to go home yesterday." I flashed a playful grin, already reaching for a cup to mark his drink order down. *Damn. Way to sound witty, Andy.*

"No, still today, I'm afraid," Dr. Hottie said with a light chuckle. "My son here has a dentist appointment in ten minutes. I figured this would be a good time to treat myself and settle the nerves." Dr. Hottie made my heart skip a beat when he looked straight into my eyes as he spoke. For once, his phone was nowhere to be seen and his attention was focused entirely on me. Okay, that was a stretch. So maybe he wasn't so much riveted on me as he was trying to look anywhere but at the surly-looking kid standing beside him.

"And who's this? I haven't seen you before, have I? I know I haven't because I never forget a face." I turned with a smile to the kid, trying not to wince when I noticed the rapidly swelling shiner on his right eye.

Ignoring my question, Dr. Hottie tilted his head in the direction Prince Charming had taken off. "Should you really be mentioning religion at work? I hope you won't be getting in trouble with your boss over that; you seem like a nice guy."

I was confused for a second. "Who mentioned religion?"

"You literally just did," the kid said with an exaggerated

eye roll. "You totally told that dick in front of us that he needed Jesus."

I snickered at that one. "No, that's not what I said, but now that you mention it, I see where it could sound that way. I didn't say Jesus as in the holy son of God—I said Jeebus. He's the canine incarnation of Satan personified, and just exactly the kind of character a charmer like that needs to meet. So yeah, totes not a religious statement... unless he worships Satan; in that case, I should probably keep him away from Jeebus. But enough about him, he's fake news. Tell me what I can get you boys to drink." I leaned over the counter to get a better look at the kid's face. "Are you okay, honey? That looks downright painful."

The kid shrugged and mumbled that he was fine while Dr. Hottie spoke over him, glancing at his watch as if remembering the time. "My son was in a fight at school. He'll be okay. How about my usual and something iced and non-caffeinated for the kiddo?"

"Do you like caramel, vanilla, or chocolate, boo-boo bear?" I asked the kid.

"Caramel and vanilla, if you can mix them," he muttered, taking a half-step away from his dad. Tracy took the cup from my hand and went to work making their drinks while I grabbed a ziplock and filled it with ice. I slid it over the counter with a wink and a sympathetic smile. "At least put this on your eye for me, boo-boo. You're making me hurt from just watching that puppy swell."

Dr. Hottie did a double take and glanced guiltily at his son. "Grayson just needs to learn that this is why we use our words, not our fists. But thank you for the ice pack."

The kid, Grayson, rolled his eyes and looked away after picking up the ice pack and putting it to his eye. Dr. Hottie sighed, shaking his head as he passed me a twenty to cover their drinks. "Single parent problems, Andy. I don't recommend it." He took the change I offered and shoved it into the tip jar before picking up the drinks Tracy was setting on the counter. "I'll see you two tomorrow. Right now, we have a tooth to save."

I nodded at his words, flashing a smile to Grayson as they turned to leave. "Keep that ice on there as long as you can, boo-boo. It will help get that swelling down."

"Wow. That sucks. Dr. Hottie finally speaks, only to reveal his baggage, am I right?" Tracy almost sounded sad as we watched the two of them walk away.

"I don't know that I would call a kid baggage. I kinda just wanted to hug them both, didn't you? Especially that sweet kid. And maybe help him wipe away that smudged eyeliner. Raccoon eyes are just a crime if you're not doing a walk of shame, honey." I turned to Tracy, a smile slowly covering my face as a thought occurred to me. "Hey, did you catch the part where he totally knew my name?"

Tracy stared pointedly at my name tag then back up at my face. "Sure, we'll go with him knowing your name, babe."

"Whatever, skank. Jelly much?" I wrinkled my nose to let

her know she wasn't as cute as she thought she was. "Besides, I got some important info in that little exchange —Dr. Hottie is single." I gave her a hip bump and turned to greet an approaching customer, whistling to myself as I got back to work.

4

CORBIN

"You're lucky I'm even talking to you right now, you big jerk. I can't believe you and Gray stopped for coffee in the lobby and you couldn't be bothered to bring one to your so-called bestie. And here I squeezed you in to save your son's tooth, too. Some friend you are, Corbin Davis." Dana playfully glared across the desk at me, her eyes narrowing at my coffee cup.

As tempting as it was to go back downstairs and get her a drink—and maybe flirt with the adorable guy at the coffee cart instead of sitting here waiting for my son to get a tooth fixed—I settled for a playful pout instead. "I'm sorry, babe. My mind was scattered. This shit with Gray has me all turned around. This is the third fight in two months. It's not like him; you know that as well as I do. I tried talking to him at the school, but it was like screaming into the void for all the reaction I got."

Dana sat forward in her chair, putting an elbow on the desk to rest her chin on a palm. "Has he said anything about the fight? Becca hasn't told me everything about what's been going on either, but you and I both know that something has to be at the root of all these fights lately, right?"

"Shit, no. He won't talk to me. How the hell am I supposed to know why he's acting out, Dana? And he knows better than to fight! And of all people to fight, what the hell was he thinking to pick some bulldozer of a kid to tangle with? He's lucky he only had one tooth knocked out if he got punched by Baby Huey back there." I shook my head in frustration, setting my coffee down to lean back in my chair.

Flipping her long, blond hair over a shoulder, Dana sat up again, fixing a pointed smile at me. "*Exactly*, honey. Think about that for a second. You know Gray better than anyone; does this whole fighting thing really sound like him? My mom instincts say there's a lot more going on than you realize."

Hearing more in the undercurrent of what she wasn't saying than in her actual words, I tipped my head to the side with a raised brow. "What do you know that I don't, Dana? I hope you're not holding anything back on me."

Reaching across the desk, Dana smiled gently as she squeezed my hand. "Drop by my house in the morning before work, after the kids have left for school. I don't really know anything yet, but I have a few suspicions. I'll see what I can get out of Becca tonight and then we'll have a cup of coffee while I fill you in on a few things tomorrow if all goes well with the intel gathering." She pulled her hand back with a frown as if suddenly remembering something. Her eyes narrowing as she wagged a finger at me, Dana shifted right into lecture mode. "And Corb? If you really tried talking to him down at the school, then I don't blame the kid for having an attitude. You of all people should know better than to put your teenaged son on the spot in public. I wouldn't have talked to your sorry ass either. Please tell me that's not what you did."

I winced, reluctantly nodding that yes, that was indeed what had happened. "I was just so pissed off when I got there. And he was doing that thing where he stares at the floor instead of making eye contact. I didn't pay attention to who was around while I ripped into him for fighting again. Probably not one of my best moments, huh?"

Dana snorted. "I'll say. Just tell me it was only the secretary there, right? I mean, I hate that skinny little bitch, but who the hell cares what she thinks."

I bit my lip, shaking my head. "That Clark Danvers kid was there too, the one he'd gotten in the fight with? And the nurse, and yes, the snippy secretary..." My voice trailed off with a sigh. "Shit. I totally screwed the pooch on that one, didn't I?"

"Oh, no. You didn't just screw the pooch, sweetie. You

went and knocked that bitch up." Dana reached out and patted my hand, her eyes sparkling with amusement. "But that's okay, we all screw up. Just learn from it and do better next time."

We continued chatting until a dazed-looking Gray came out a few minutes later, his cheek puffed out with a piece of gauze dangling from the corner of his mouth. He stared off into the distance, obviously still a little out of it from whatever they'd given him to numb the pain, while the nurse handed me care instructions. After I thanked them for their time and paid the bill, I guided him out of the office so we could go home.

We were halfway home when I stopped at a red light and noticed McDonald's on the next corner. It occurred to me that the kid wouldn't be able to eat tonight, so when the light changed, I decided an impromptu stop at Mickey D's was in order. After we picked up our food from the drive-thru, I pulled into a parking spot at the far end of the lot where we'd have privacy to eat. Gray looked curious as he took his shake, mumbling unintelligibly around the gauze.

I shrugged, easily understanding what he was trying to ask. "I figured we'd eat here since we both know that McDonald's fries have roughly five point three minutes between being hot enough to burn the taste buds off your tongue and too cold to be edible. Shove the straw in the other side of your mouth after the shake thaws a little, and you should be able to get it down without killing your mouth. Drink up, because that's your dinner. You don't want to suck too hard and damage the work the dentist just did on your mouth, so go easy."

Gray nodded, setting the shake between his thighs as he leaned his head back against the seat, staring out the windshield while I rustled in the bag to dig out my food. I spoke calmly while I unwrapped my quarter pounder, carefully keeping my focus on the food and off Gray.

"Remember our old car rules, bud? Right now, we're in the cone of silence. We can say anything here without fear of judgment. If you're not bleeding anymore, why don't you pull out the gauze and talk to me. I'd like to understand what's going on with you, kiddo. I feel like maybe you and I aren't communicating as well as we could be these days."

Several minutes of silence went by while I nonchalantly ate my burger and fries as Gray thought about what I'd said. Eventually, he pulled the gauze out and dropped it in the empty bag, wincing when he took his first drink of the milkshake. I kept eating, content to let him find his own equilibrium and decide whether to speak or not. My patience paid off a few minutes later when he shrugged and muttered under his breath, "It doesn't matter. You wouldn't understand anyway."

My heart broke a little at that. How had we gotten to a place where my own son didn't think I'd understand what was happening in his life? When my mouth was too full to comment, Gray took a deep breath and shrugged. "I'm sorry for fighting, Dad. I know you don't like it when I do that, but I couldn't help it this time."

I swallowed what was in my mouth, pausing to dab my mouth with a napkin before answering. "Was it self-defense? Because that kid was pretty big, dude. I'd like to think you're smarter than to fight him by choice."

Gray huffed out a laugh. "Nobody would ever choose to fight Clark Danvers."

"That's not really an answer," I chided gently. "Look. I get it, kiddo. Nobody wants to be a narc. But realize that if you don't talk about whatever's going on with you, then I can't fix it."

Banging the back of his head against the seat, Grayson groaned with frustration. "That's just it, Dad. I don't want you to *fix* anything! Don't you realize that I'm not a baby? I'm fifteen now, practically a man."

Keeping my voice steady, I hid my amusement at him banging his head like a toddler throwing a tantrum while announcing that he wasn't a baby. "Oo-kay. What *do* you want me to do then, Gray? I need you to tell me what you want from me, son."

He turned to look at me, holding my gaze for several seconds before swallowing audibly with a terse nod. "Just be on my side, okay? Can you just do that?"

"I can do that," I said, reaching up to ruffle his hair and brush it out of his eyes. "How about we go home before your pain meds wear off? We could hang out and ignore the world for a while. Maybe even play a little Destiny, if you want."

Gray's eyes danced as he grinned, flinching away from my hand and looking in the side mirror to fix his hair. "Sure, we can do that—as long as you don't start crying like a little girl when you get your butt handed to you."

5

ANDY

I was muttering under my breath after Gam-Gam's nurse, Helen, left for the day. "Stupid, lazy-ass cow. This is what we get for accepting help from a state agency. I can't believe she couldn't even be bothered to at least give Gams a can of soup, Jeebus. I bet she didn't feed you either; did she, boy?"

Devil dog looked up at me with an indignant sniff, bumping his head against my shin before leading me over to his empty food bowl. He stared pitifully into it with a whimper as if to show me just how badly he'd been mistreated in my absence. He growled when I scratched between his ears, snapping at my hand as I reached for the food dish.

"Easy there, Satan." I tutted as I took his bowl to wash it and get his dinner ready. "I'm obviously the only able-bodied person around here who gives enough of a shit about your ass to make sure that you eat, so maybe you might try being a little bit nicer?"

He tilted his head to the side, showing me the blank side of his face where his empty eye socket had been sewn shut at birth—his version of telling me to talk to the paw. After I set his dish down and stole another scratch between his ears, I washed my hands and pulled a casserole out of the freezer. Once it was heating in the microwave, I wandered down the hall looking for Gam-Gam.

I started to call out when I entered her bedroom, but the unmistakable, cloying scent of cigarette smoke kept me from announcing myself. I crept silently toward the bathroom, swinging the door open with a flourish. "Busted! Your ass has been caught in the act, old lady."

Gam-Gam clutched her heart with her free hand, glaring up at me with a startled frown from where she was crouched fully clothed over the toilet, sneaking a cigarette. "Goddammit, princess! Are you trying to make me have another episode? That's the kind of bullshit that puts someone with a faulty ticker back in the hospital. What the hell is wrong with you, brat? What if I'd been taking a shit or something when you walked in? I swear, your generation has no manners at all. You're lucky I'm dressed, now that I'm thinking of it. Next time you might not be so lucky."

"There'd best not *be* a next time." Rolling my eyes, I walked forward and plucked the cigarette out of her hand, tossing it into the toilet and flushing. "That's what's wrong with me." I pointed at the swirling cigarette butt that was refusing to go down. "Dammit, Gam-Gam. You know better than to smoke. Where did you get your hands on cigarettes again, anyway? I thought I'd found all your stashes. And for the record, if you'd been taking a shit, it would've smelled a little better in here than the fumes from that nasty old coffin-nail you were burning did."

Gam-Gam giggled girlishly. "Quit being a nicotine Nazi. And as for my stashes? Never ask a lady to give up her secrets, princess. Now come on, help a weak old lady to her chair." She reached for my arm, fumbling feebly as if having a hard time staying upright.

"I bet you are weak, after putting those toxic pollutants into your lungs. What the hell's the matter with you, Gams? Are you wanting to spend another summer in the hospital? Maybe this time we can go for a triple bypass, hmm? That is, if the reaper doesn't take your sneaky ass first." Even while I huffed, I was still wrapping her hand around my arm and carefully guiding her out to the living room.

"Are we going to have another lecture, or are we going to settle in with our dinner and watch our show? We're up to episode nine, I believe." Gam-Gam smiled up at me as I helped her into the chair.

Shaking my head, I groaned playfully. "Are you seriously trying to change the subject by distracting me with a baking show? Really? Of course we're going to watch our show, but what's the point of rooting for who you want to win if you don't plan to be alive to see it happen? Every time you smoke a cigarette, you're taking another three minutes off your life, and you don't have that many left to spare, old woman." When Gam-Gam started to glare, I held up my hands. "I'm done, the lecture is over—until next time."

I handed her the remote to get our show started and went to get our food out of the microwave. Once I had our dinner plated, I carried the dishes in and set up a TV tray for each of us. Before I took my seat in the chair alongside Gams', I grabbed our matching bedazzled snuggies and tucked one over her lap, pulling the TV tray closer for her. Once I was settled and appropriately snuggled in, I grabbed my own tray and put my feet up while the bake-off began to play.

We ate in peace while we watched our show. Even the devil dog left us alone during the dinner hour. Instead, Jeebus contented himself to lie at Gams' feet while she ate, in an attempt to pretend he was a good boy. Halfway through the show, Gams banged her fork and knife against the empty plate, snorting indignantly as she pushed the tray away from her. "That idiot judge is swayed by the rack on that young chickadee. You know damn well that our guy's fondant work was much smoother than that cow's. There's no way she deserved a higher score."

"True, his fondant was good. But the judges said his cake was dry. It doesn't matter how pretty the display is if it's not edible," I said as I set my own empty plate aside.

"Balderdash. Eduardo's cake was clinging to that bastard's fork while Mary Beth's was crumbling everywhere. Anybody knows that crumbling is a sure sign of a dry cake, honey. She's obviously boinking him for points," Gams said with an indignant snort.

I knew from experience not to argue with her when she was likely correct, so I gave up. "You're right, Gams. I must've missed that part with the crumbs." I bit back a yawn, snuggling under my blanket more as I leaned back in the chair. I groaned when I saw her staring at me with a conniving look in her eyes. "What now, woman? Can't you see I'm plumb worn out? I'm too tired for any more of your hijinks today."

"You're tired because your life is all work and no play, princess. You need to get out and find yourself a man. Don't think I didn't catch you eyeing my little Eduardo during the show. Let's give it some thought; do we know anybody with a single son? I bet I do if I think about it hard enough." Her fingers tapped a rhythm on the arm of the chair, her eyes narrowed in thought as she mentally shifted through the name of every possible gay man in her acquaintance. "Oh! Well lookie there, I've already thought of at least four interesting candidates. In fact, I think Helen mentioned having a gay nephew. Maybe I could see if she has a picture on her phone."

Yeah, I need to shut that shit right down. "No, I'm just tired because I had a long day at work. And for the record, what red-blooded person wouldn't eyeball Eduardo? He's a hottie, even for a twink. Not usually my type, but I have eyes, don't I? Why else would he have been cast on the show if he weren't adorable? Besides," I crossed my fingers as I blurted out a bold-faced lie, "I'm already seeing someone, so you don't need to try setting me up with anybody."

Gams perked up in her chair, clapping her hands as she focused the entirety of her attention completely on me again. *Ah, fuckballs. Here we go.* "You're seeing somebody? And this is the first I'm hearing of it? That's it. I've heard enough. You'll need to bring him to dinner. Nobody gets to court my only grandchild without my seal of approval."

I ignored the rest of her statement, going for the old sidetrack move instead of responding to the dinner invitation for my nonexistent boyfriend. Holding up my hand, I ticked off my responses with my fingers. "You don't have to approve of who I date, I'm not being courted, and I'm also not your only grandchild, Gams. Have you forgotten about Sheila? I *do* have a sister, you know."

Gams bared her teeth, a feral growl not unlike devil dog's coming out of her throat. "No. That little skank is no grandchild of mine. When she apologizes for being stupid and aligning herself with the wrong side of history, then maybe I'll consider forgiving her. Until then, she's dead to me."

I reached over and rested my hand over Gams' drumming fingers, trying not to think about my conservative, homophobic sister who hadn't spoken to me since the day my family had ever-so-sweetly invited me to hit the bricks on my eighteenth birthday, *bless their hearts*. I blinked back tears as I smiled briefly at the fierce woman who'd been the only one in my family to have my back. "That's okay, Gams. I don't need her ass, anyway. You, me, and Beelzebub are a team, right? We've got all the family we need right here under this roof."

"Damn straight," Gams said, then tipped her head with a curious expression as she stared at me for a moment. "Although maybe straight isn't the right word if we're talking about a team that includes your prancing ass, princess."

Shaking my head, I leaned over the arms of our chairs and kissed her wrinkled cheek. "I swear you need to spend less time with that devil dog of yours. You just get meaner every day, old lady."

6

CORBIN

I couldn't help but smile as I watched Dana go through her familiar routine of prepping her perfect cup of tea. I was on my second cup of coffee before she finally lifted the cup with both hands, closing her eyes rapturously as if saying a prayer of thanksgiving while she took her first sip.

After she'd set her cup down and began to eye the tray of pastries like a predator, I knew the conversation was ready to commence. She shook her head and reluctantly looked away from the baked goods. Fighting the urge to glance at my watch while I watched her do the old dance of pretending she didn't want the sugary carbs, I kept my focus on the reason I was here. "So did you get any good intel for me last night?"

Dana closed her eyes again and nodded before pensively gazing back up at me. Her expressive topaz-colored eyes were filled with concern. "Yes, and I need you to prepare yourself, because this might be a shocker. This is going to involve a little bit of show and tell to get the point across, so get ready." She bent and picked up a battered gray duffel bag from beneath the table. Setting it on the chair between us, she unzipped it and pulled out a lacy pink T-shirt.

"So Becca is turning into a girly-girl after all this time, huh? Let me guess... there's a boy involved." I couldn't figure out what my friend's tomboy daughter's fashion choices had to do with Gray, but I figured she'd get there eventually.

Dana shook her head. "Nope. Well, not exactly. This does involve a boy, but not like you're thinking, and that's the thing I need you to understand. Becca is holding these for a friend—Gray, to be exact. Apparently, she takes one in her backpack when he asks, so he can change into it once they get to school." Setting the shirt on the table, she proceeded to pull out more articles of clothing, each one frillier and more delicate looking than the one before it.

I stared blankly at the clothes, my brain struggling to compute what I was hearing. "Wait... I don't get it. What are you saying? Are you trying to tell me that my fifteen-year-old son is a cross-dresser? Where did he even get these?"

"Don't be an idiot, Corb. I'm going out on a limb by sharing this with you, because that's what we do—we help each other. We single parents have to be in this together, right? You have one chance to get things right with him, so don't fuck it up by throwing around terms like cross-dressing. And as for how he got them? His allowance and the mall would be my best guess. Or Amazon. Never discount the old one-click option."

Setting my coffee down, I leaned forward and picked up a ruffled lilac-colored tank top she'd pulled out. "Okay, then explain it. And please speak really slow and make it simple enough for my idiot brain to comprehend. I don't care what the hell he is or isn't, but I have a right to know what's happening with my own kid. Hell, I don't give a shit what he wears. I'll send the kid to summer camp at RuPaul's place if that's what he wants. But I can't do anything if I don't know what's going on."

Dana rolled her eyes. "Oh. Em. Gee. And they say women are the drama queens. Listen closely and let me break it down for you, Poindexter. Grayson is coming to terms with his identity. He hasn't changed his pronouns yet, according to Becca, but he's now identifying as nonbinary, or enby for short. This is causing problems at school, and it's the reason he's being bullied and getting into fights. Becca told me that Danvers kid has started calling Grayson by a girl's name, Gracie. He taunts him in front of the whole school by calling him Lacey Gracie."

"Are you fucking kidding me right now? What a little prick! And the school is letting him get away with this shit?" I sat back in my chair, my fingers stroking the ruffled neckline of the tank as I considered this new information. Dana let me sit there and process for a few minutes while she quietly put the clothes back in the bag. After a moment, I reluctantly passed her the tank and waved a hand toward the bag. "What I don't understand is why is he hiding this from me?"

After setting the bag back under the table, Dana picked her tea up and looked off to the side while she took a sip, as if considering her choice of words. "He's a kid, Corb, filled with all the teen angst and hormones on top of this new journey of self-discovery. Maybe it's not so much that he's hiding it from you, as it is a matter of him simply not knowing how to begin the conversation. You and I both know what a life-altering moment it is when someone begins to realize and accept that maybe they weren't the person they'd always thought they were. I don't know much about the subject yet, but I do intend to educate myself further."

"What, are you trying to say that you're not an expert on everything LGBT? That is how nonbinary is classified, right? He's under the rainbow blanket now?" I drained my coffee cup and reached for the carafe to refill it. "I'm bisexual, and I've never hidden it. You'd think that of all people, he'd know he could open up to me. It's not like I'm some homophobic shit-stain on the underwear of society or something. I know what it's like to have people judge you."

Dana waved a hand in front of her face as she giggled. "Shit-stains and underwear. Thanks for that appetizing image." Taking a breath, she set her tea down and looked longingly at the pastry plate. "There's only one problem with what you said, Corb. I don't know that Grayson actually knows you're bi. Has he ever even seen you date a woman, let alone another man? You keep your private life locked down tight, so how would he know? Or have you guys had that talk and I'm not aware of it?"

I thought for a moment and realized that there was a strong possibility that Dana had a point. "You know what? Maybe he doesn't know. I've never talked about any of my exes, male or female. We spent so many years mourning Maria before I dated again, and it's not like I was going to bring someone I was seeing around my son if it was just casual." I leaned back with a heavy sigh, crossing my arms over my chest as I gazed back at my best friend. "So what should I do? Come out to him and hope he does the same? Or maybe I could just take this bag home and leave it on the kitchen table?"

"Yeah, sure. Out Becca for talking and take away the one person he trusts. Because that's a solid plan—not." Dana rolled her eyes, huffing out an exasperated breath while she shook her head at me. She finally reached over to the pastries and snatched up a cherry Danish. "Why don't you try having some guy talk with him? Let it evolve naturally. Have you helped him shave yet? Would you guys even do that? My mom had this whole moment with me when I shaved my legs for the first time, is that something you men do too? Maybe you could help him shave and offer up a few makeup tips about not letting his foundation get caked into the stubble or something."

I threw my head back with a bark of laughter. "I'm pretty sure that if I tried to have a Kumbaya moment where I taught him to shave, Gray would start looking around for hidden cameras. Especially if I tried to give him makeup tips. What the hell do I know about makeup?" I paused for a beat then looked back at her curiously. "Wait. Are you saying that Gray's wearing makeup too?"

Dana shot me a scathing look, complete with a skeptically lifted brow, that said she was questioning my intelligence. "Did you not see the raccoon eyes he was sporting when you brought him for his appointment? There was smeared eyeliner and mascara all around his eyes. I don't know if he wears it often, but he sure as shit had at least eye makeup on yesterday."

"Oh yeah…" I said slowly as a light bulb went off in my head. "I almost noticed that at the school until the whole tooth thing came up. After that, I must've just clocked it as being part of his black eye. So makeup, huh?" I let my voice trail off for a moment then looked up at Dana with my best puppy dog eyes. "I don't suppose you could give him a few makeup tips, could you? I'm definitely not qualified for that discussion."

"Uh-uh. Sorry, Charlie. Not my job." She smiled as she spoke, as if to soften the blow. "Honestly? I would totally have that conversation with Gray if it came up, but I think this could be a real bonding moment for the two of you. So what if you don't know about makeup? Watch a YouTube video or three. Hell, do whatever you have to do to get him to talk to you. Just don't let him put cake makeup over his baby whiskers—make sure he knows to start with a smooth palette."

I held up my hands. "But that's just it, how can I get him to talk to me about makeup when he's keeping this major part of himself a secret? Before we can bond, he has to be willing to confide in me. Honestly, Dana. Tell me the truth —what am I doing wrong that my kid won't talk to me? If Maria were alive, this wouldn't have happened. She would have known. Something like this never would've snuck up on that woman."

Dana smiled softly, her eyes crinkling at the corners as if fondly remembering my late wife. "Don't sell yourself short, Corb. Maria wasn't psychic, she just paid attention. All parents have their strengths and weaknesses, but it's all an uphill ride with no GPS—I don't care who you are, raising kids isn't easy. All you can do is your best. Talk to him and get him to open up to you. Hell, maybe buy him some makeup and mention the raccoon eyes from yesterday? That could be an opening, if you're brave enough to put it out there like that."

I took a deep breath, raking a hand through my hair before dropping it to my lap. "I just can't wrap my brain around this whole thing. I do need to Google it, I know that much. I'm sure there are a lot of websites that'll tell me everything I need to know about what it means to be— what did you call it? Enby? Hell, it would be easier if he had plans to become a drag queen or something. Now that

I could've shared knowledge about, since I've known a few of them in my day." I looked up at her hopefully. "Wait. Do you think maybe he might be interested in becoming a drag queen? I could probably help him with that, if it's that simple."

"Honey, he's not trying to become a drag queen, or cross-dresser, or anything else your cis-male brain is trying to conjecture. He likely doesn't identify as a particular gender. He obviously identifies as gender neutral, but how much of that is masculine or feminine, and whether that percentage changes on a given day? I think from the sounds of it, he's more genderfluid, but those are things that only Gray can tell you. If you want him to open up to you, you'll need to learn the lingo. And while you're at it, drop the whole drag queen and cross-dressing idea. That's one way to guarantee that he'll never talk if you come at him with stupid shit like that." Dana snorted, muttering something about my heteronormative stupidity as she picked up her tea to take a sip. *So much for her not knowing much on the subject yet.*

"Fair enough," I said after a moment's thought. "It'd be so much easier if I could just get him to talk to me. Hey, speaking of drag queens though... have you been to your brother-in-law's bar lately? I wonder if he still does those drag queen shows once a week. We had a blast when we went to that benefit last summer, and I'm pretty sure the flyer said they do it every Thursday. Do you talk to Nick very often? Maybe you could find out for me. Hell, I bet one of those gorgeous queens would be a great help with all this, now that I think about it. They're not always femme, only when they're in character. The rest of the time they're just normal guys, right? Some are femme, some aren't, I think. At any rate, I'm sure one of them would help me be able to understand."

Dana dropped her teacup onto the saucer with a loud clatter, her eyes narrowing as she wagged a finger in my direction. "Enough with the drag queens, Corbin! How many times do I have to tell you? That's not what nonbinary is about. Quit being a fucking idiot before I have to smack the stupid off you." She passed her phone across the table, a website already open on the browser with the familiar rainbow flag proudly unfurled across the top of the page. "I haven't had time to read it thoroughly; I was looking at that before you got here. Enby, as I said, means not fully identifying as either gender binary. Enby people can place themselves anywhere on the spectrum of masc to femme, and sometimes neither. You'll have to let Gray lead the way and figure it out for himself. He'll let you know when he's ready."

Picking up the phone, I scrolled through the site, making a mental note of the web address. "We can talk about this until we're blue in the face, Dana. But he's still not talking to me about it, and that's not okay for me as a parent. How can I help him if he won't talk? And for the record, I'm not talking about going to drag night because I'm confusing nonbinary with cross-dressing or drag queens in general, I'm just looking for answers. If I can get one of them to talk to me, maybe they can help me figure out how to open the lines of communication with Gray. That's all I was thinking." I passed back the phone with a guilty grin. "I'm really not a *complete* idiot, you know."

Dana's eyes sparkled as her lips slowly spread into a knowing smile. "No, but in this case I'm starting to think that maybe *I'm* the idiot. It occurs to me that you're looking for an excuse to hit drag night, aren't you? Why wouldn't you just say that, you big doofus? And yes, Nick still does drag nights every Thursday. You do you, babe. If you want to hit up Saint's Place tomorrow for the show, I can have Becca invite Gray to spend the night here with us. You're past due for a night out anyway." She flashed me a wink as she picked up her cup. "Who knows, maybe you'll even meet someone."

7

ANDY

Sucking in my cheeks, I made a perfect fish-lipped pout while I focused on contouring my cheekbones. My nemesis, Princesse Fetish, caught my eyes in the mirror. She stood behind me in fishnets and a bra while sliding her hip pads in place. "Whatchu lookin' at, girl? Don't be jelly because I can work these curves."

Setting the brush down, I turned my head from side to side to make sure everything was even before reaching for my false eyelashes. "Why would I be jealous of your wannabe curves, Princesse? I can hit up the dollar store for those cheap-as-hell foam pads you use any time I want." I flashed her a wink and tilted onto one hip, slapping my round ass. "When you've been blessed with your own juicy rump roast, you don't need to stuff your pantyhose with foam discs. Run away with your spindly self, little fish. Let this dusted queen show you how to shine."

Princesse raised her eyebrows so high they nearly touched

her hairline as she spoke in a sugary-sweet voice that was faker than her tangled-looking weave. "Is that what we're calling your fat ass now? Juicy? No, *honey*. That's called too many carbs and not enough cardio. Seriously, baby girl. Eat a salad—please. And as for dusted? I believe the word you meant to use was busted, *honey*."

"Enough, ladies. The show starts in ten; I don't need you working my nerves and getting me all upset." We both turned to see Honey Combover glaring at us from the table beside mine. "Both of you need to pull in your claws and play nice. Honestly, I do not have time for this drama, and I sure as hell don't want you to get me sweating from last-minute stress. The last thing this queen needs is another tape malfunction."

I smiled apologetically at my drag mother. Her campy makeup was on point, playing well against the scruffy, salt-and-pepper beard that framed her round jawline. Honey's hairy chest highlighted the décolletage she'd created with the hardworking red velvet corset that was somehow managing to hold everything in place. Her ruby-red lipstick was a perfect match to the corset, but what really tied her look together was the frizzy, blond Dolly Parton wig she'd been pinning into place when we'd so rudely interrupted her.

Princesse showed her low IQ as she stupidly gave Honey a bold once-over. "The tape malfunctions happen because you don't properly tuck, Honey. I'm telling you, queen. The boat tape Miss Precious uses is the only thing strong enough to handle whatever swampy mildewed shit you've got going on down there. I mean, how many times do we have to tell you? You gotta wax that ragged birds' nest, girl. Maybe try washing with some antibacterial soap and powder that stanky taint before you tuck and tape."

Honey spun on her stool, her nostrils flaring as she slowly rose to every inch of her six-foot-four-inch height while still in stocking feet. Princesse took a step to the side, moving around and effectively putting me between the two of them while Honey glowered down at her. "Listen, hunty." Honey's voice was deceptively calm as she leaned over me to handle the princess. "You know I love you, girl. But if you want to start throwing shade, then the library is open. Would you care for reading, Princesse?"

Shaking her head quickly, Princesse held up both hands. "No tea, no shade necessary. Forgive me, Mama Honey. My blood sugar is a little low and a girl gets hangry. You know how it is."

"Then eat a damn Snickers and keep your bitchy snark to yourself, Miss Thang. Run along now and finish getting ready so you can slay tonight." Honey held both hands up, palms down as she flicked her fingers toward Princesse. "You heard me, get that bony ass moving. Your table is on the other side of the room—you don't even belong over here getting all up in my space. *Bye, Felicia.*"

While Princesse scrambled away, Honey met my eyes in the mirror as we both busted out laughing. Neither of us had missed the unsightly rip in her fishnets, revealing the pimpled thigh directly beneath her left buttcheek. Honey bent from the waist to press her cheek against mine as she murmured in a low voice, "I should really tell her, right? I mean, it's probably the Christian thing to do, don't you think?"

I snickered as I fluttered my false lashes to make sure they were firmly attached and not going to stick. "Good thing we're a fine couple of heathens, so we're off the hook when it comes to that little snake in the grass. If hunty wants to get shady, then she gets what she gets."

"*Meow*, baby girl." Honey winked and blew me a kiss as she stood straight again. As she turned to retake her seat, I winced at the glittery black micro-mini she was wearing. Damn, if there was a tape malfunction tonight, there'd be no hiding that shit. Honey untucked was not easily hidden. And in a scrap of material that barely covered her naughty bits? Yeah, she'd be turning the party up.

"All right, ladies. Tell me my queens are ready to slay." We all turned at the sound of a new voice in the room to see Nick St. Cloud walk into our dressing room, only to find himself immediately surrounded by a swarm of fawning baby queens.

The former Navy SEAL turned barman was sex on a stick. As the owner of Saint's Place, he was fiercely protective of all of us and had made this our Thursday night haven. Even though he was flirty and never failed to make a girl feel good, he put off a vibe that showed him to be completely unavailable—not for lack of trying on any of our parts. I didn't know his story, but I was pretty sure his heart had already been given to another.

"Don't even think about it, baby girl," Honey murmured when she spotted me licking my lips while I mentally undressed him. "That boy is off the shelf and we all know it."

"All I'm saying is I don't see a ring on his finger or anyone warming his bed on a cold night. I just need him to open that door a crack and I'll wriggle right in there." I waggled my eyebrows for effect and picked up my blond, ponytailed wig.

"And what would your ass know about whether his bed is warmed or not? Baby girl, that door's not just shut, it's locked and barred. Besides, what are you even doing thinking about St. Nick when all you ever talk about is that Dr. Hottie you serve coffee to every day?" Mama Honey smiled smugly at the stricken look that crossed my face. "Uh-huh, that's what I thought. Now be a good girl and finish getting ready."

Honey bent to put on her stilettos while I finished making myself look like a young, pseudo-virginal Britney Spears. By the time I was done, the dressing room was half empty and the show was already in progress. Jonny, one of the sweet stagehands who blushed every time one of us flirted with him, stuck his head around the doorway. "Are you ready, Kandi? You're up next."

"You know it, sweet cheeks." I grinned at the red flush that slowly spread over his cheeks as I flounced toward him. "Kandi is here and ready to work it, bitch."

I grabbed my glittery pink skateboard and popped a piece of bubblegum into my mouth to make my grand entrance as they called my name. Gliding on the skateboard with one foot curved up behind me to give the audience a flash of what was hiding beneath my schoolgirl skirt, I waved cheekily and blew a bubble as I came onstage. I hopped off and expertly kicked it to the side as the opening line of "Oops, I Did It Again" came blaring over the speakers. By the end of the song, I'd ditched my innocent white blouse with the Peter Pan collar and was wearing an emerald-green bikini top with a matching fringe of shimmering beads hanging from the band.

Kicking off my shoes, I knew damn well that I looked like a teen boy's wet dream in my short Catholic school skirt and white tights. The beads slid and bounced against my toned abs with every perfectly choreographed booty shake as the song changed. I owned the stage as I danced around, lip-synching my way through "Work Bitch." The crowd gasped as I turned my back to them, shaking my rump as I bent to smile at them from between my legs while mouthing the next line: *See me come and you can hear my sound.* Touching my hand to the floor, I twerked a few times before executing the bend and snap as I spun to face them again.

The crowd went wild as I went through my routine flawlessly, thank you very much. Right as I did the death drop onto my back and turned onto my side, sliding one stocking foot over my inner calf while slowly gliding the back of my hand along my side to maximum effect, I made the mistake of looking past the front row.

I almost choked on my bubblegum when I saw who was sitting at the bar. Rolling onto my back again, I lifted my feet in the air and pretended I was pedaling a bicycle while my brain quietly malfunctioned. What the hell was Dr. Hottie doing at my show? Did he know who I was? Muscle memory alone took me through the rest of my routine, but the whole time I was firmly aware of those familiar gray eyes following my every move.

8

CORBIN

"See something you like up there, Doc?" Nick grinned as he slid a pint across the counter to me.

I grinned back, waving a hand to gesture toward the stage. "I'm wondering if I'm a perv for being turned on by a version of teen Britney. Hey, do you know her? What's her real name? I feel like I know her from somewhere, but I can't put my finger on it."

"Kandi? Yeah, I'd say you probably do know her, given where you work. Sorry, bud. I can't reveal a queen's identity, even to a friend. If she wants you to know, she'll have to be the one to tell you." He grinned as he wiped down the bar with a wet rag. "So tell me, Doc. What brings you to PTL night? You're not one of our regulars. In fact, I was a little surprised to even see you here."

Did the people in this town really think that I was some

stuck-up prick? Or more likely, did I give off a straight vibe? I took a drink of my brew, wondering if maybe I'd been a little more in the closet than I'd realized. But then again, unless people saw me dating a man, my entire life had been a constant coming-out party to everybody I knew. Pushing that aside for the moment, I latched onto what he'd said. "PTL? What, are we meant to be praising the Lord for our glorious queens?"

Nick threw his head back with a shout of laughter. "Dumb-ass. Not that kind of PTL. This one stands for Properly Tucked Ladies—get it right."

I grinned at the acronym's true meaning. "I love it. PTL... that's a good one."

Tipping his head toward the stage, Nick asked his question again. "Seriously, though. What brings you in on a Thursday? Were you curious? Because curiosity killed the cat, you know—or made its straight tail curve a little. Not that you can't be straight and enjoy a good drag show."

I groaned at the bad pun. "Okay, let's just get this out there. Hello, my name is Corbin and I'm bisexual. Happy? As for what I'm doing here, I was at your benefit last summer and had a blast. I thought maybe I'd drop in and check it out on a regular night."

Nick winced. "Sorry, man. That was a dick move on my part. I didn't mean to make you out yourself there. I had no idea."

Waving a hand, I shook my head to let him know it didn't bother me. "Unless you'd seen me with a man, how would you have known? It's not like it's tattooed on my forehead. As far as you knew, I'm a widower with a kid. Don't even worry about it, Nick. We're good, I promise. Shit, I don't even think about it myself half the time. I've never been one to let my sexuality define me. I like who I like, whatever form they come in. I just hope I'm raising Gray the right way so he'll get that one day."

"I'm sure you are, man. Parenting ain't for wimps, that's for sure. Speaking of your kid, how is Grayson? Is he still thick as thieves with my niece, Becca? Maybe you and Dana should keep an eye on that shit now that they're getting older." He quit wiping the bar to lean against it while we chatted.

"I don't think that's a concern right now, to be honest. That's actually part of what got me to come in here. Dana got some intel for me out of Becca because this week Gray had his third fight in the past two months. It's not like him, you know? Turns out, he's being bullied because he's identifying as nonbinary, and apparently Becca smuggles in pretty clothes and makeup for him to wear at school. So yeah, he's got more on his mind right now than girls—or boys, for that matter. As I'm quickly finding out, I have no idea what he's into right now."

Nick blew out a breath. "Enby, huh? That's gotta be tough at his age. Teens are such little dickwads sometimes. Let me guess, you had no idea about the bullying either?"

"Not a clue," I admitted sadly. "And here I've been busting his chops for fighting all this time. I probably don't need to tell you how shitty I felt when I heard the truth. Anyway, Dana thought I was crazy, but I figured maybe one of the PTLs here could help me wrap my brain around the whole thing. Or hell, if nothing else, maybe offer some makeup tips that I can use to get him talking? He has no idea that I know, and I'm trying to figure out how to start the discussion."

"Dana wasn't wrong, that was a crazy idea. Hell, half of these queens would chew you up and spit you out if you approached them with questions like that if they didn't know you." Nick nodded toward the table area where Kandi was making her way through the crowd, collecting tips. "You know what? Kandi is just the gal for you. She's a darling little Southern belle, and sweeter than that sugary tea they drink." He waved a hand to get Kandi's attention.

I nearly swallowed my tongue as she approached with a bright smile. If she'd been hot as hell on stage, then she was on-fucking-fire in person. Nick motioned in my direction. "Kandi, come here, honey. I want you to meet my buddy, Corbin. He needs to talk to someone about his kid and you're the only one I'd trust with a favor like that. Be nice now, his son's family to me."

Kandi tittered, her bright green eyes roaming over my body before finally settling on my face. "Oh, sweetie. Miss Kandi will happily do any favor for you, just name it," she purred in a soft voice.

Fuck me. I squirmed on the bar stool, trying to readjust without being obvious when my pants tightened. Sending a silent apology to my cock, I reminded myself that it would have to wait its turn. No matter how turned on I was, I was here to find help for Gray, not get laid.

"Easy now, you're going to make my buddy pass out if you lay it on so thick, girlfriend. Mere mortals are no match for your fabulosity, remember?" Nick said, chuckling again as Kandi stepped closer, coming to a stop almost between my knees.

Finding my voice, I blurted out the thought that had been rattling through my addled brain. "Where do I know you from? I do know you, right? You recognize me, don't you?"

Kandi seemed to deflate a little, her persona dropping somewhat as she leaned against the counter and regarded me thoughtfully for a moment. When she spoke in a normal voice, my jaw dropped. "Large, triple-shot Americano with a dash of cinnamon."

I was so stunned, it took me a moment to react. "You're Andy! You're the cutie who works at the coffee cart inside the medical plaza."

A slow smile spread over her face as Kandi preened. "I'm well aware of where I work, doll face. But if you're gonna call me cutie, then we can definitely talk. How about you buy me a cup of coffee at the diner next door after I change? Sit tight, and I'll be back out so we can talk about this favor you have in mind."

I nodded dumbly, still not quite able to speak. As she blew me a quick kiss before flitting away, Nick started laughing again. "Oh, shit. You're totally screwed, Doc. If you can't even hold a simple conversation with her, that little queen's gonna wrap you around her perfectly manicured pinky finger."

9

ANDY

Mama Honey had left the building. Or at least her drag persona had. Larry grinned at me as I patted his shoulder on my way to my own dressing table. He was packing away Mama Honey's makeup and cleaning up his area. "Hey, baby girl. Did you catch Princesse Fetish's low market tuna tonight? We probably should've told her about those torn fishnets. I'm not even throwing shade, I kind of felt bad for her busted ass when she turned her back to the audience to do a little snap and bend and they totally split. I swear, girl, I gagged in all the best ways—it was that shocking."

I turned to Larry with a loud gasp. "Shut your piehole! Are you being serious right now?" I groaned with disappointment at the sight of his gleeful nod. "Dammit, I totally missed it. Seeing that would've given me life. For real... like in a deeply fulfilling way. And then I'd have a good excuse to offer her some Clearasil for those thigh zits." Pulling off my wig, I reverently placed my crowning glory on its stand before reaching for coconut oil and a cotton ball. Time was of the essence and I needed to remove my eyelashes before I could attack the makeup.

Larry watched me work for a few seconds before he leaned forward and planted his palms on his knees with a meddlesome smile. "Sooo..." He spoke slowly, drawing out the word. "I happened to glance over at the bar on my way back and I saw you talking to Nick and a very interesting-looking hunk of man. Care to share what that was about?"

Closing one eye, I pressed the oil-soaked cotton ball to the eyelash glue while glancing back at Larry in my mirror. "That interesting-looking man would be a certain Dr. Hottie."

His eyebrows shot to his hairline as Larry jerked back with a dropped jaw. "That was the one and only Dr. Hottie? The man who stars in all your wet dreams? He was here in our little club? Guuurl..." He fanned his face with a hand, blinking rapidly as if he were about to faint.

I snorted and shifted the cotton ball to the other eye, my attention focused on removing the lashes I'd just loosened while I talked. "Right? Nick pulled me over to introduce us and I about died. I mean, can you even? And get this, he's waiting for me right now. We're going out for coffee so he can ask me a favor." When Larry gasped again, I stifled a giggle and focused on my eyelashes. "No, it's nothing like that, perv. Apparently it's something to do with his kid. Nick asked me to be nice to him because the kid's family."

"Oh, I bet you'll be *real nice* to him, honey." Larry cackled while he scratched the thick stubble on the side of his jaw.

"It's not like that," I said again, wincing at the sting when I removed the second set of lashes a moment too soon. "Okay. It may be a *little* bit like that? But holy shitballs. I'm about to have a private tête-à-tête with Dr. Hottie. I mean, damn. Jesus, Mary, and Joseph. Tell me how the hell I'm supposed to sit across the table from him and drink coffee like a normal person without drooling all over myself or trying to dry hump him or something? Help me, Larry. I am not equipped for this scenario."

The sound of Larry's rich, deep-throated laugh warmed my heart and settled my nerves a tad. "First of all, didn't you say he wanted to talk to you about his kid or something? Calm down, girl. Breathe for a minute. Remember, just because he came to see our show doesn't mean he's not straight. And we all know what happens when we fall in love with those cute and oh-so-tempting straight boys, right?"

Our eyes met as we spoke our mantra in unison. "Poor little queer hearts get broken when they pine for straight boys."

While I went to work removing my makeup, I eyed Larry thoughtfully in the mirror. "The thing is, I'm not sure if he *is* straight. At least, not razor-edged straight anyway. Trust me, Miss Kandi knows when a man is inspecting the merchandise and liking what he sees, and he was definitely interested in what I was selling. Oh! Wait! No, my gawd! I left out the best part! He was trying to place me, so I rattled off his coffee order in my normal voice and he was all like... *wait!* You're Andy, the cutie from the coffee cart!"

Larry nodded thoughtfully. "Yeah, calling you cutie doesn't sound totally straight, I'll give you that one. You should definitely get the four-one-one on him, because you never know. How fantastic would it be if your crush was interested in return?" He sniffed, wiping away an imaginary tear. "My heart is full now. Just think, my sweet little gurl with a man of her own to love and hump in both good times and hornier, for as long as you both shall lust."

I started giggling at that, but before I could answer, my phone rang and the screen filled with my grandmother's beautiful smile. "Hold that thought, Larry. Gam-Gam's calling." Larry smiled fondly and sat back while I answered the call, putting it on speaker so I could continue deconstructing my look while we talked. "Hey, gorgeous. Are you calling to see if I fell on my ass tonight, or are you headed to bed?"

"I know you didn't fall on your ass, or I'd have heard the damn caterwauling from here. No, Jeebus and me are turning in for the night and I thought I'd give you a poke and let you know that it's okay if you don't want to come home tonight. Seeing as how you have a boyfriend and all, I thought maybe you'd have other plans. Maybe for a nightcap and a little winkie-wink?" I winced at the intrigued look on Larry's face at Gams' insinuation. "He did come to see the show, right? Any beau worth his salt would be there to cheer his main squeeze on, especially if he's courting you like a proper gentleman."

Flipping my middle finger up at Larry's snort, I avoided eye contact with him, puffing out a cheek and rubbing harder with the makeup remover wipe. "He was here, and yes, we have plans for coffee. I'm trying to get undone and into my street clothes right now because he's waiting for me at the bar. And Gams? Please never say winkie-wink again. That's disturbing on too many levels."

"Well, hell. Why didn't you lead with the fact that he's there, you big dodo? Look at you, letting me ramble on while your man waits for you. What's wrong with you, princess? Hurry up, don't you dare keep your man waiting. Save that for when you want to tease him, baby. But don't forget to make plans to bring him for dinner one night, you hear?" She paused after giving her order, her voice softening. "Have a good time, sweetie. You deserve to have fun and be young for a change. I'll see you in the morning. Now don't let me keep you. I want you to go out and have a good time. Love you!"

"I love you too, Gams. Sleep well." Setting my phone aside, I rubbed moisturizer over my face and gave my hair a fluff, hoping Larry would let it go.

Right, because that would happen. Larry pounced almost soon as I ended the call. "Am I correct to assume that your grandmother believes the esteemed Dr. Hottie to be your boyfriend? Spill the tea, darlin'. I'm all ears and just dying to hear this one."

Rising from the stool, I removed my panties then spread my legs and squatted so I could remove the tape from my dick and finally untuck the family jewels. Larry leaned back against his dressing table, crossing his arms over his chest. "*I'm waiting*," he said in a singsong voice. "Why does your grandmother think you might not be coming home tonight, Kandi-Andy? It's adorable that you actually seem to think you're going to get away without explaining that to me."

Now that I was free balling it again, I sat back down, mirroring Larry's position as I leaned against my own dressing table with a nice, wide manspread to let my dangly bits air for a minute before I got dressed. "It just kinda happened." I looked over at Larry with a wince. "You don't understand what it's like, big guy. She's so worried about me being perpetually single that she was getting ready to start setting me up with any and all comers."

"Honey, if your gams knows good comers then you can just tell her to send them my way," Larry said with a deadpan face. He shook his head, looking a little more serious after a moment. "Andy, making up a fake boyfriend for your gams is gonna come back and bite you in the ass. You do know that, right? She's a smart little cookie. If she finds out you tried to pull one over on her, she's gonna kick your ass six ways from Sunday."

"Nah, she'll just sick her demonic dog on me." I snickered then stood up with a sigh as I reached for my bikini briefs.

"I know it was a bad idea, but it came out of my mouth before my editor had a chance to stop it from happening. And now she wants me to invite him for dinner? This is a fuckin' mess. What am I gonna do, Larry?"

While I wiggled a pair of faded blue skinny jeans on—ones that were tight enough to see my religion—Larry worked his jaw from side to side as he thought about my problem. I finished dressing and paused to smile at the faded whiskers effect on either side of my nicely displayed bulge. This had been a perfect night to wear my favorite pair of come-for-Jesus pants. I turned to look at my ass in the mirror, smiling in satisfaction when I saw that yes, it still looked fabulously perky.

Larry grunted, rolling his eyes as he watched me preen. "Yes, you look good, darlin'. Quit obsessing. We both know you're working those britches. So here's what I'm thinking —you said Nick mentioned something about Dr. Hottie needing a favor? Right there's your answer. Offer him a little swap action. His favor for yours."

I glanced up at Larry in confusion. "What favor do I need to swap?"

Larry rolled his eyes so hard I'd swear I almost heard his sockets pop. "Gurl. Seriously? What were we *just* talking about?" Larry snapped his fingers a couple times in front of my face. "Wake up, buttercup. Get with the program. You're obviously in need of a fake boyfriend. Depending on how large his favor is, maybe you guys can work out a little trade." He paused and waggled his eyebrows for effect. "And while you're at it, don't be shy about offering up any other favors, if you know what I mean."

Fanning my face with a hand, I blew out a breath. "Boy howdy, do I know what you mean. But crap on a cracker, how would I even offer something like that?" I turned around and got to work cleaning up my table when I realized that too much time was passing and Dr. Hottie—Corbin—was waiting for me.

Larry smiled like the Cheshire Cat as he answered. "Simple, darlin'. Talk to the man. And if the opportunity presents itself, go with it. We both know you're not shy, so don't go playing the ingénue with your hot doc. If all else fails, channel Miss Kandi—that bitch won't let you down." Larry stood and waited while I gave my dressing table one last once-over before rising to join him.

I felt like a little kid next to my hulking friend as we made our way through the dressing room. When we walked back out to the bar area, Larry draped an arm around my shoulders and gave me a squeeze. "I'll let you introduce me next time; I have a friend of my own waiting at the bar. Do me a favor? Be your best, sassy self and have a good time. He who hesitates, defecates—and don't nobody need more shit in their lives."

After Larry left me with a final pat on the back, I made my way over to Corbin. The fact that he was checking me out as I walked up didn't escape me. This new version of Dr. Hottie was such a difference from the morning customer who never looked up from his cell phone that I wasn't quite sure how to even begin to deal with this turn of events. Taking a deep breath, I charged over with a bright smile. "I'm back! So, you said something about a cup of coffee?"

I looked around the nearly empty diner, my eyes roaming over the faded artwork on the wall, the cracked Formica tabletop, the scarred linoleum, the selection of pies spinning around inside the rotating display case—yeah, I was pretty much looking at anything other than the delicious specimen of masculinity sitting across from me.

After our waitress dropped off the slices of cherry pie we'd ordered when we'd been seated and filled our cups with a substance resembling coffee, I had no choice but to find my balls and face him. When I looked up, I found Corbin watching me with a bemused smile. I bit my lip almost shyly before speaking. "What? Does it weird you out to be around me now that you know about my alter ego?"

Corbin shook his head as he picked up his fork and cut into his pie. "No, it's stranger to be sitting here with the guy who serves my morning coffee than it was to watch you in drag. Thank you, by the way, for taking the time to do this with me."

My nerves faded as we began to talk. "No trouble. If I'm being honest..." I leaned forward with a conspiratorial smile. "I work up quite an appetite when I do my routine.

A little pie and coffee will hit the spot right now. If we weren't here, I would've been heading home with a rumbly tummy. Maybe you're the one doing me the favor, if you think about it. Speaking of favors, what was it you wanted from me? Nick mentioned something about your kid?"

Corbin dropped his fork with a clatter, leaning back in the booth and dropping his hands to his lap. "I feel really stupid now that we're sitting here. I don't want you to think that I'm an idiot or something."

I cocked my head to the side, gazing at him curiously. "Why would you ever think that? Now you have to tell me what's up; I'll curl up and die of curiosity if you don't."

Puffing his cheeks out, Corbin blew out a breath and gave a slight nod. "You noticed my son's black eye the other day, remember? So it turns out that he's being bullied because he identifies as enby—that's short for nonbinary. Have you heard of that?" He paused and waited while I resisted the urge to say *duh* and simply nodded instead as I took a bite of pie. Corbin blew out another breath, raking a hand through his short hair. "I don't know why I thought that a drag queen might have any clue about what an enby might be dealing with, but I was hoping to pick your brain about it and... I don't know... maybe get some makeup tips or something?"

I resisted the urge to laugh—almost. Corbin chuckled when he saw the suppressed laughter in my eyes and I couldn't help but laugh along with him. "Yeah, I definitely don't identify as anything other than masculine. I can see where people might be confused since I do tend to be flamboyant and glamorous in my daily life, but you have to understand me when I tell you that I don't identify as anything other than a cisgender man. Drag is just a way for me to let my hair down and get into my creative side. I'm sure it could be confusing, from the outside looking in. My drag mama is an old-school gender-bender type of queen. He doesn't bother to shave his thick stubble or his hairy, manly chest—even when he is in full-on Honey Combover regalia."

Corbin nodded thoughtfully. "At the risk of sounding like a complete idiot, can I ask what you mean by cisgender?"

"Wow, you really don't know much yet, do you? Have you and your son even talked about it?" I paused when I realized I hadn't answered his question. "Simply put, cisgender means that my sense of personal identity and gender matches my birth sex. Yes, I am a totally gay drag queen, but I personally identify completely on the masculine spectrum, if that makes sense." Corbin's confused expression made me snort. "Yeah, yeah, yeah. I get it. I'm a totes fab gay man who loves lip gloss and knows my way around a mani-pedi. That doesn't make me female; that makes me effeminate, sure. But honey, trust me when I tell you that I am one hundred percent man, which makes me cisgender because I identify as the gender I was assigned at birth."

"Oh! I remember reading that word, now that you explain it. Yes, that does help a little. Sorry, I'm really new to this whole conversation. I've got so many new terms rolling around my brain from the websites I've been reading since I found out about my son's identity yesterday that my head is still spinning." He stopped and got that bemused smile again. "I guess it's a good thing I haven't talked to my son about it yet?"

After taking a sip of my coffee, I set the cup back down with a barely suppressed shudder at the bitter taste. "If you haven't talked to him about it, then how did you find out?" I doctored the motor oil trying to pass itself off as coffee with cream and sugar while he told me about his best friend and how she'd helped him figure out what was going on.

I nodded and hummed at the pertinent parts of his tale, then circled back to the whole makeup thing he'd mentioned when we'd first sat down. "And you want me to give you makeup tips for him? How is that supposed to work, hon? I don't understand where you're going with that. If he doesn't know that you know that he's nonbinary and wearing makeup, how exactly are you planning to start offering makeup tips? Are you planning to just toss it out casually over dinner? *Pass the corn, son. Oh, and have you seen the new MAC line? The Glitter Tripper collection is bomb.*" I paused to laugh at that idea before continuing. "Besides, won't he think it's weird coming from you? Unless you were wanting me to come give him makeup tips? Cuz that wouldn't be weird, right? I'm sorry, but I'm still trying to figure out what the favor was that you wanted in the first place."

Corbin slumped against the booth with a heavy sigh. "Yeah, as you can tell, I didn't think this out too well. Obviously I'm the last person he'd want to get makeup tips from. You say MAC and I'm thinking trucks, but I'm pretty sure you're talking about cosmetics, right? And while you're undoubtedly the perfect person to help him, if I'm being completely honest, he might freak out if we tell him that I came to ask you for help when he's yet to tell me himself. How would I even explain that one? Fuck. You know what? Maybe Dana was right, and this was a bad idea."

I held up a hand to stop him before he went full emo on me. "Honey, hush. Although, I should probably explain that most drag makeup is completely different than regular makeup. Ours is more theatrical because it's stage makeup. But I do use some regular makeup in my own routine, and as you witnessed at my job the other day, I do adore a good sparkly lip gloss." I shot him a rueful grin and circled my finger as I pointed at him. "Tell me this, Corbin. Does he even know that you're bi? That is what you are, right? Wait. Don't say anything. It's awkward for me to have assumed things about your sexuality. Never mind, forget I said anything," I said as I quickly began backpedaling.

Corbin froze in his seat, his mouth falling open for a moment before he seemed to gather himself. "Um. No, I'm pretty sure that Gray doesn't know I'm bisexual. Is it obvious? The way people have been asking me lately, I was starting to think I might need to tattoo the bi pride flag on my forehead."

"Please, do that. Oh, honey. Those colors would really bring out your eyes," I said, pouting prettily for effect. I grinned at the way his cheeks pinked up, then waved a hand to dismiss it and get back on track. "Sweetie, you've always presented as straight to me, if I'm being honest— that is, you did until you called me cutie and stared at my assets." I flashed him a wink, biting back a smile at the blush that spread over his cheeks again. I wanted to swoon on the spot. Lawd have mercy, it was too damn cute to see this studly man blush.

He pulled his coffee closer, wrapping his hands around the mug and staring into the inky blackness as he quietly brought the conversation back around and let my flirty business pass. "About the bi thing though. It's really never come up and I don't think he's known anything about me dating since his mom died. I haven't been in a serious relationship and it wasn't like I was going to bring a casual date around my kid, you know? It's entirely possible that he has no idea. I mean, it's not like I've talked to him about my exes from before I married his mother."

"I'm sorry for your loss," I said softly. "How long have you been a widower, if you don't mind my asking?"

He was quiet for a moment before glancing up to catch my eye with a soft smile. "No, I don't mind talking about Maria. It's been nine years now. Grayson was six years old when he lost his mother." I opened my mouth to ask how she'd passed, but he simply held up a hand as if anticipating my question. "It was pancreatic cancer."

We sat there silently for several beats while I turned everything around in my head. Thinking about my own predicament and Larry's suggestion, I drummed my fingertips on the table for a moment then glanced up to find Corbin watching me with those gorgeous gray eyes of his. "What if I were to offer you a favor trade type of deal? This might sound a little crazy, but I seem to be in the market for a fake boyfriend to appease my crazy gam-gam's meddlesome matchmaking. What if I pretended to be your boyfriend, and was open with your son about my drag persona? Maybe that could get him to talk. And bonus, if he sees you with a man, you won't have to get that tattoo. I bet if he thought we were together, he'd feel a lot better about opening up to you. In fact, I'd almost guarantee it."

Corbin rubbed a hand over his jaw, blinking slowly as he mulled over my offer. "I'm probably completely insane, but that sounds almost crazy enough to work. What would I have to do to fulfill my end of the bargain? It feels like you'd be the one doing all the work here, since I have the most benefit if this builds a bridge between me and my son."

I snickered, shaking my head as I pictured my gams and her satanic ball of fluff. "Trust me, hon. You'd be doing me just as big a favor. All you'd have to do is come have dinner at my house and pretend to be my boyfriend for a night. Or longer, if we need to let the fake relationship run its course. Hell, you can even bring Grayson along. Gams would love that. I gotta tell you, you'd be doing me just as big a favor as I'd be doing you if you can get my gams off my ass about the whole boyfriend thing."

Corbin raised his coffee cup, extending his hand as if to toast. When I lifted mine and clinked our cups together, he shot me a goofy grin. "This is probably one of the most unorthodox schemes I've ever heard of, but it might just be crazy enough to work. So, do we need pet names?"

Fluttering my lashes, I smiled flirtatiously. "Oh, honey. You always need pet names."

10

CORBIN

A week later, I still wasn't entirely sure how it had happened. But now that I apparently had a fake boyfriend, I figured it would be stupid to waste any more time before I put our plan in motion. Other than a little flirtation every morning at the coffee cart, so far nothing had changed between us, and no further mention of how we'd proceed had come up.

Until today, that is, when Andy mentioned the whole dinner with his grandmother thing. That had told me I couldn't put this off any longer. Not to mention the fact that I was chafing at the bit to have things out in the open with Gray. The idea that he was hiding such a major piece of himself from me was unsettling, to say the least. As his parent, I wanted to be a part of his life in every way—but especially with something as important as his sense of identity.

After Mandy was kind enough to rearrange my afternoon,

I decided to surprise Gray by picking him up from school. Thanks to the new information I possessed about his gender identity, it wasn't surprising when I saw a flash of pink under his open hoodie when he came walking out, chatting with Becca and completely oblivious to my presence. I watched as Becca first noticed me, then elbowed Gray before leaning into him and whispering something in his ear. In a flash, he was zipping his hoodie while looking from side to side as if to see where I was parked until she pointed me out.

Motioning for the kids to come over to the car, I rolled down the passenger window. "I was in the neighborhood. Can I interest you two in a ride home?"

Before Gray could answer, Becca was already opening the car door and sliding into the back seat. "Hi, Dr. Davis. This is a nice surprise," she said politely while Gray got into the passenger seat beside me.

He looked a little disgruntled as he buckled his seatbelt. When he saw me watching, Gray flushed and looked away as he spoke. "Why are you here picking us up? I didn't get into trouble today and I always walk home with Becca. Is something wrong, Dad?" He sounded nervous and uncertain, but it was hard to tell for sure when he was staring out his window rather than looking in my direction.

I took a steadying breath and pulled out of the school parking lot. "No, nothing's wrong, son. But we do need to talk." Gray turned to look at me then. I could feel the tension radiating from him as I turned into the neighborhood and headed toward Becca's house to drop her off first. Shaking my head, I held up a hand and quickly reassured him. "It's not about you, Gray." I chuckled nervously, rolling my neck and second-guessing my having brought this up in front of Becca. I'd thought having her there as a buffer would be good, but maybe not so much. God, I sucked at this parenting shit sometimes.

"What is it, Dad? Just tell me whatever it is, because you're kinda freaking me out here." Gray glanced at Becca over his shoulder as if looking for support.

Trying again, I decided to just put it out there. "Sorry, son. I didn't mean to alarm you. It's just that I've been seeing someone, and I thought maybe it was time for you to finally meet them."

My statement was met with dead silence. Several moments went by before Gray spoke up. "Wait, you're dating? You never date. Besides, aren't you too old for that now?"

The laughter that bubbled out of my chest almost instantly calmed my nerves. Shaking my head, I took my eyes off the road long enough to shoot him a playful glare. "Excuse you? I'm only thirty-six, brat. That's hardly old, and I'm definitely not dead. And yes, of course I date. I've just never wanted to bring casual dates around you, especially when you were younger. But this one is getting a little deeper than past ones have, and I figured maybe it was time for you to meet each other."

Gray drummed his fingers against his thighs as that sank in. "Okay, that makes sense. I get it. What's so different about this chick then?"

Taking another breath, I stole a glance in his direction. "Well, for starters—he's definitely not a chick."

After another few moments of dead silence, Gray blurted a nervous laugh. "Wait, you can't be dating a dude. You're not gay. You were married to Mom." He said this in such a befuddled tone, it was hard not to laugh.

Lifting a brow, I shot him a wry grin. "Son, surely your generation isn't unaware that there are multiple levels on the Kinsey scale, yeah?"

Gray scratched his head. "The what scale? What are you even talking about, Dad?"

Becca leaned forward, giggling as she tapped Gray on the shoulder. "Dude, really? The Kinsey scale is the rating system that goes from totally straight all the way to completely gay. There are a lot of steps in between. I think your dad is trying to tell you that he's bi. *Duh*."

When Gray turned to look at me in shock, I grinned. "What she said. Seriously, Gray, it's never occurred to me that you didn't know that about me. I've dated both genders ever since I was your age. I hope you don't mind that I'm bi, because that might be weird for both of us if that's the case."

Shaking his head, Gray was quick to respond. "Mind?

No, if anything, I think it's cool. It's a little weird that I didn't know, but heck—I didn't know you were dating anybody, male or female. I guess it would probably be just as freaky if you were dating a woman after all this time." He paused for a moment, then shot me a shy smile. "Thanks for telling me, Dad. I'll be happy to meet your boyfriend."

And just like that, he moved on and everything went back to normal as the two of them started chattering about glee club tryouts, and my big coming-out moment passed like it was no big deal. Joining the conversation, I cleared my throat and asked about the tryouts. "So, the glee club, huh? That sounds like fun."

As Gray excitedly began to tell me about the tryouts they'd done today and how they both were hoping they'd made it, I breathed a sigh of relief. Andy had already helped me turn a corner with my son just by giving me a way to open up about myself to him. It wasn't much, but it was a start. Maybe if I'd found the courage to bring Andy up sooner, I'd have known he was trying out today.

After we dropped Becca off, Gray brought the conversation back to my supposed boyfriend. "What's his name, Dad? And when were you planning to introduce us?"

"His name is Andy, and you've already kind of met him, actually. He's the guy who gave you the ice pack at the coffee cart last week. And I was thinking that maybe we could invite him over for dinner tomorrow or the next night, if that's okay with you." I spoke casually, following Gray's lead and trying not to make a big deal out of it.

"That guy's your boyfriend? Wow, you guys were totally cool about it. Like, totally on the down low. I wouldn't have even guessed you knew each other, let alone that you were dating by how casual you were in front of me." I winced inwardly at the truth of his statement but kept a smile on my face as I shrugged. Gray drummed his fingers against his thighs again as he continued his thought. "Actually, it totally makes sense now that I know he's your boyfriend. I can kinda see you guys together. Yeah, you should invite him over tomorrow night, if you can. He seemed pretty chill. Especially the way he dealt with that homophobic douchebag that didn't like his lip gloss."

"Alrighty then, I'll check with him and see if it works with his schedule." Our conversation ended as I pulled into our driveway, but rather than taking off and heading to his room when we went inside like he usually would, Gray continued hanging out with me. He sat at the table and pulled out his homework while I considered what to cook for dinner.

As I went to work chopping vegetables for a stir-fry, all I could think was—*bless you, Andy*. Our fake relationship had already begun to work with bringing me and Gray closer to a common ground. Gray looked up with a smile when he heard me humming contentedly.

Damn. Having a fake boyfriend was already turning out to be the best idea I'd never had. Hmm. Should I buy him flowers or something before our "date" tomorrow? Shit. I probably should've gotten his number by now. If I had, I could've texted him about tomorrow night instead of springing it on him in the morning. Hopefully he wouldn't mind that I was starting out as a crappy fake boyfriend in that regard.

11

———

ANDY

"Don't look now, but here comes your *faux-beau*." Tracy flashed me a mischievous grin as she tried to beat me to the cash register.

"Slow your roll, Miss Thang. I never should've told you my little secret." I smacked her on the butt while giving her a hip-check to shove her aside. I was standing in my rightful place behind the register when Corbin made it to the counter. "Hey, boyfriend," I greeted with a saucy wink.

Corbin shoved his phone into his pocket. I heartily approved of this small change in his morning routine. "Good morning, sweetheart." He paused with a wince. "No, scratch that. Honey? Baby? Babe? Help me out here, Andy. Just tell me what to call you."

Tracy shoved up behind me, resting her chin on my shoulder. "I'm pretty sure you can call him anything you want, and he'll come." She pinched me in the side and gave a perfect Beavis laugh. "*Heh-heh-heh*. I said come. And yes, the pun was totally intended."

I shoved her back with a roll of my shoulder. "Run away, hussy. I swear the mess that comes out of your mouth is enough to make a preacher cuss." Lifting my chin, I stared down at her with my haughtiest look. "This is a place of business, young lady, not a locker room—thank you very much."

Corbin chuckled at our now familiar act. "I swear you two could have your own reality show. But enough about that, I have a little favor to ask, Andy."

I tilted my head toward the espresso machine. "Tracy, would you mind making my sexy boyfriend his morning java fix while he tells me what the latest favor is that he needs from little ol' me?"

"Already on it," Tracy chirped as she snagged a cup from the stack and got to work.

When I turned back to Corbin, I smiled at the sweet flush spreading over his cheeks. "Uh-oh. You're blushing, Doc. How bad is this favor?" I leaned forward and cupped a hand around my mouth to stage-whisper. "And more importantly, will we need lube?"

The tension in his shoulders relaxed as Corbin began chuckling. "I certainly hope not. The thing is, and it's okay if you say no, but... I kinda told Gray about us and we want you to come to dinner tonight." Before I could answer, he held up both hands and talked a little faster. "I know it's last minute and I really should've asked you sooner. I would've texted, but we haven't exchanged numbers. We should have each other's numbers if we are supposedly dating, right? Shit, I'm a sucky boyfriend."

He was so cute, I couldn't bear the thought of embarrassing him by laughing, but damn did he make it hard. I swallowed my giggle and held out a hand, wiggling my fingers impatiently. "Give me your phone, please."

Corbin looked confused as he dug out his phone and obediently placed it in my palm. Resisting the urge to roll my eyes, I held it back out to him. "Unlock the screen, boo." There went that blush again. His cheeks were bright red as he pressed his thumb to the screen to unlock it. I sent myself a quick text, then held it up and pouted as I took a selfie. After I'd saved the number and created a new contact for myself, I passed it back. "There you go, now your fabulous boyfriend is in your phone. I'm not opposed to pervy late-night calls with heavy breathing, but remember a diva needs her beauty sleep, m'kay? I would've made myself your number one speed dial, but I'm assuming that spot belongs to Gray, so I went with number two."

"Okay, that's perfect." He shoved his phone away without looking at the text, shooting me a bemused smile instead. "So, about that dinner invitation..."

"Did I forget to say yes?" I slapped my hands to my cheeks,

Home Alone style. "Oh, honey. It's not only a yes, but I will be there with bells on."

Tracy scooted around me to set Corbin's coffee on the counter. "I should warn you that he's probably not using that as an expression—our Andy may very well show up wearing bells somewhere on his person."

Corbin blinked a few times then glanced back at me with a dazed smile. "You will have more than just bells on though, right? Remember that Gray will be there too."

"Lord have mercy. You're gonna kill me dead if you don't quit taking everything so seriously, boo. What time do you want me there, and make sure you text me your address— you can't say you don't have a way to contact me now," I said with another sassy wink.

"Is six o'clock okay?" He scratched the back of his head, somehow managing to look more adorable. "We can always do it a little later if that doesn't work for you. Like I said, I'm aware that this is awfully last-minute."

I waved a dismissive hand. "Hush. I don't have anything else going on, and I'm off work at four. That gives me plenty of time to run on home and check on my gam-gam before I come over. But you need to quit apologizing, you hear? You're fine, boo. It's nice to know that you Davis boys are so excited to get me over to your house that you can't stand waiting long enough to schedule it out a few days. That's how I choose to look at it, so don't you dare take that from me."

Corbin grinned as he reached for his wallet. "Alrighty then. I guess I'll see you at six."

"That you will, boo. Now put that away, your money's no good here anymore." I blew an air kiss as I motioned toward his wallet. "Your boyfriend works here, remember? I have it on the authority of the day manager that you are not to be charged."

Tracy snorted. "Says the day manager himself. Talk about an abuse of power. Unless, of course, you're planning to trade his morning coffee for sexual favors, because that's an idea I could get behind."

"Sure you could," I replied with a laugh. "You're just hoping to cash in on that little program when Michael shows up this afternoon."

"You know it." Tracy bumped her hips against mine. "*Heyyy.*"

"Yasss, queen!" I laughed and bumped her back while Corbin sipped his coffee and watched us with an amused grin. I blew him another kiss. "Don't worry, boo. No reciprocal favors are necessary to get your morning caffeine fix." I waggled my eyebrows, dropping my voice to a purr. "Those would fall under the grateful tip category anyway."

Tracy bent over double, grabbing her stomach as she sputtered. "He said just the tip!"

Corbin chuckled as he took a step back, his cheeks

blushing a bright pink again. "On that note, I think I'd better get up to my office. See you tonight?"

"Definitely," I said, flashing him a final wink before I turned to wag my finger at Tracy. "Girlfriend, I should slap you silly for that shit. Instead, I think I'm gonna dream up some payback for when Michael shows up later."

Tracy gasped. "You wouldn't!"

"Honey, hush. It's like you don't even know me," I intoned sadly as I turned with a smile to greet an approaching customer. Damn, I loved my job.

❖

I didn't get nervous until I was actually standing on Corbin's front porch. The suburban home looked like it belonged on one of those old TV shows like *Leave It to Beaver* or some shit. The doormat even said "Welcome to the Davis Abode." Planters filled with gerbera daisies hung over the pretty white banisters that framed the porch area. There was even a damn swing hanging in front of the large picture window that stood to the left of the door. This wasn't the house of a cheap trick on a Saturday night—this was a home where a real family lived.

I took a deep breath and channeled my inner diva as I knocked on the door, sending a silent prayer to the benevolent goddesses Cher, Madonna, and Lady Gaga to help me through this little charade.

When the door swung open, Gray was the one to greet me. He looked completely different than he had the first time I'd laid eyes on him. Despite the hoodie he wore that was practically zipped to his neck, he seemed relaxed and welcomed me with a friendly smile. "Hey, there. It's Andy, right? Come on in, my dad's in the kitchen."

"Well, I see your eye healed nicely. No offense, boo-boo, but you looked like something the cat dragged in the last time I laid eyes on you." I was already relaxing as I followed him into the house and he closed the door behind us. I glanced around the homey living room, unsurprised to see the same traditional-style decor that had been promised from the exterior. "Nice place. I was just thinking that your house looks like something out of a sitcom from the fifties. You know what I mean, like the setting of a perfect home?"

Gray looked around as if seeing the place for the first time. He nodded slowly and flashed me a grin. "Yeah, it kinda does, doesn't it?" A shadow of sadness flashed in his eyes as he shrugged. "This was how my mom decorated the place. I guess me and Dad never got around to changing it. I dunno, it's just home, you know?"

I nodded with understanding as I paused to look at old family pictures that hung on the walls. "There's nothing wrong with that, boo-boo. If it ain't broke, don't fix it, am I right? Besides, there's a lot to be said for classic decor. Your mom had good taste, because I have to say—your home is lovely."

"Thanks," Gray said, smiling happily at the nod to his mother.

I racked my brain for a second, looking for another topic. When I remembered something Corbin had mentioned about Gray's school while we'd been flirting one morning this week, I latched on that. "So your dad says you tried out for glee. That's cool. How's that working out?"

Gray's smile disappeared as he shook his head. "Fu-I mean, screw that. Because I've been involved in multiple disciplinary infractions this semester, I'm not eligible for any extracurricular activities. I guess I forgot to tell my dad that part."

"Darn tootin'. If you'd told your dad, I bet he'd have been all over that school's ass. I mean, he still could, if you wanted? I feel like he'd love to go take them on."

"Nah, I'm over it. Becca was only doing it for me, so we're both gonna just do our own thing this year. Maybe learn guitar from YouTube or something." He shrugged like it was no biggie, but the pain in his eyes said differently.

Motioning toward his hoodie, I asked the question I already knew the answer to. "What's with having your hoodie zipped so high in a warm house? Aren't you feeling flushed? I know I would be." As I said that, I shrugged off my own jacket and hung it on a coat rack that was conveniently standing in the entryway.

Gray blushed harder and mumbled something about not having had time to change after school. "So what? You're home now, why not take it off? Who cares what's under that hoodie?" I pushed, intent on doing my part to repay Corbin's favor.

The kid would never open up if he wasn't given an opportunity. I felt a little bad about it, because I didn't want to shove him out into the open if he didn't want to come out. But on the other hand, I figured that he was old enough to tell me to fuck off if he wanted. It's not like I was trying to strip the kid bare, I was just providing him with an opportunity to share if he wanted... and mentally crossing my fingers he'd take me up on it.

He shrugged and unzipped it a little, not enough to reveal what was underneath, but at least it wasn't choking him anymore. "I'm wearing a shirt that I don't usually wear at home. I guess I got a little sidetracked talking to Dad, and yeah... because this isn't awkward, right?"

We both startled when we heard Corbin's voice from the doorway behind us. "Can I see it, Gray? I'm pretty sure you know that this is a judgment-free home, isn't it? Unless you're wearing a shirt with the Nazi flag emblazoned across it, I can't see me having a problem with anything you'd choose to put on your body."

Gray snorted. "I mean, there *is* a flag on my shirt, but definitely not that one." He took a deep breath and looked up at his dad, raw vulnerability shining from his eyes. "Promise not to freak out, okay?"

Corbin smiled gently. "Gray, if you didn't freak out when I

told you that I have a boyfriend, I'm pretty sure I can offer you the same courtesy. Listen, if you're not comfortable, you don't have to show us. But if you have something you'd like to share, I'd love to see it."

His fingers hesitated over the zipper as Gray thought about that for a moment. Then he gave a short nod and quickly unzipped his jacket, pulling the hoodie off and dropping his hands to his sides as he shyly looked back up at his father. He was wearing a gray tee with a big heart over the chest, striped with the nonbinary flag colors of yellow, white, purple, and black.

Corbin looked confused like he didn't understand the significance, so I threw him a bone and squealed with delight. "John, Paul, and Ringo! Y'all can butter my butt and call me a biscuit—I love it! That's the enby flag inside that heart, right?" I fanned a hand over my face. "I love how inclusive you are around here. Boo-boo, that shirt is life and I adore it! It's so sassy. Do you have any more? I'd love to see them."

"Umm... I guess?" Gray stole a look at his dad out of the corner of his eye, his shoulders relaxing when he saw that his dad was smiling and showing interest. "I can show you some stuff after dinner, if you want."

"If I *want*? Honey, please." I glanced at Corbin curiously, because I wasn't sure how much he'd told Gray about me. "Did your dad forget to tell you about Miss Kandi? That's my drag name, boo-boo. I perform once a week over at

Saint's Place. Ask your daddy if you don't believe me—he's seen my act."

Gray's eyes widened as his mouth dropped open. I laughed as I reached over and gently pushed up on his chin to close it. "I guess that answers that question, now doesn't it?" Hooking my arm through his, I turned us toward where Corbin was standing just inside the doorway. "Why don't we let your dad get back to whatever he was doing in the kitchen while I tell you all about it?"

Corbin discreetly mouthed a relieved *thank you* as Gray turned to lead us into the other room. I chattered away to Gray, telling him all about my drag life while Corbin went back to cooking. Gray led me over to the dining table and I finally let go of his arm when he moved to start clearing away his homework while I took a seat. He didn't really have much to say while I babbled about my favorite makeup, until I mentioned a new concealer I'd found that covered the worst zits. That's when his eyes sparked with interest as he took his own seat at the table.

"Wait, so you're not just talking about drag makeup. Are you saying that you wear regular makeup too?" He took a breath and blushed slightly as he pointed toward my mouth, as if suddenly realizing that I was wearing gloss. "Sorry. I just remembered the whole incident with your sparkly lip gloss and that douchebag who didn't like it when I met you the first time. It's probably lame of me to have even asked, right?"

I waved my hand with a shooing motion as I tittered

playfully. "Hush, boo-boo. You're fine. And yes, even when I'm not in full-on Kandi mode, I feel naked without my favorite lip glosses, and hey—a good concealer never hurt anybody. That little concoction is a gift from God, honey." I pulled out my phone and opened my gallery before passing it over. "Here, check it out. That's me as Kandi, in all my splendiferous glory."

Gray grinned as he scrolled through my gallery. "Wait... you do Britney Spears? That's awesome, man."

I glanced over at Corbin, sharing a private smile while he pretended to focus on chopping vegetables while Gray and I chatted. My heart swelled at the intimacy. A butterfly fluttered in my stomach, but I pushed that bitch down where it belonged. *This is fake, honey. Don't get attached to this family.* While Gray was distracted with my phone, I prodded a little further. "So tell me, boo-boo. What happened to your face last week?"

Gray set my phone down as he bit his lip, staring down at his lap as though deciding how much he wanted to share. When he finally looked up, he stuck his jaw out defiantly, but the haunted look in his eyes nearly broke me. "So, it's like this, okay? I mean, if Dad can be brave and talk about being bi, I guess I can share my own truth. The reason I'm wearing the flag on my shirt is because I identify as enby."

I nodded in understanding, moving right along with the conversation. "Do you have pronouns you'd prefer us to use? Or have you even gotten there yet?"

He shook his head. "No, I've thought about it. I've decided to stick with masculine pronouns even if I actually consider myself to be genderfluid. I'm not gonna judge anyone else's preferences on the subject, but for me personally, it's more comfortable leaving it like it's always been. I might change my mind when I'm older, but I want to stick with the male pronouns because that's how my mom knew me. But yeah... sometimes I feel a little girly, while other times I don't feel feminine at all and I'm totes masc. It fluctuates, if that makes sense."

"Remember that you're literally talking to a gay man who does drag, boo-boo. If it didn't make sense to me, then you might as well slap me upside the head and call me silly." I rolled my eyes for effect while Gray snickered.

"I like the way you talk," he said suddenly. "You're from the South, right? Or is that just part of your shtick?"

My eyebrows shot to my hairline as I gasped indignantly. "*Shtick?* If you were a few years older I'd tell you where you could *stick* your *shtick*, boo-boo. No, honey. I'm from a town so deep in the South that sushi is still called bait."

Corbin interrupted us as he started setting plates of food on the table. I moved to get up and offer to help, but he waved for me to stay seated. "Don't worry, I've got it. What can I offer you to drink? We've got water, juice, soda, or I could open a bottle of wine—it's your choice."

"You don't even want to see me if I'm drinking wine, boo. We haven't been together long enough for you to experience drunk Andy just yet. Plus I have to drive home later, so I'll just say no to the vino. I'm good with water," I said as I pulled my plate closer, taking a deep, appreciative whiff of the spicy-smelling enchiladas he'd prepared. "No, my gawd! I think I'm in love. For reals though, tell me this isn't fresh, homemade guacamole."

Gray was practically hugging his plate as he nodded with a wide-eyed smile. "The salsa is fresh too, that's what my dad was making when you arrived."

I jerked my head toward Corbin, looking to see where this so-called salsa was hiding. "Don't you tease me now, boo. Mexican food is the direct route to my heart. Maybe a few other places, but that's not a dinner table convo."

Corbin was chuckling as he brought a bowl of salsa and a basket of tortilla chips to the table. "I feel like I should have known that. There I go being a sucky boyfriend again."

I played along, knowing that Gray was paying close attention to our interaction. "That's okay, boo. That just gives you room to improve. If you'd started out perfect, I'd probably have put you on a pedestal—and that wouldn't be good for either one of us. It'd be exhausting and eventually disappointing for both of us, am I right?"

After he'd set glasses of water in front of each of our places, Corbin finally joined us at the table. He seemed to take a steadying breath before turning his attention to Gray. "I couldn't help but overhear your conversation, kiddo. I hope you know that I will always support you, however you identify yourself—and that also includes whoever you eventually choose to love."

Gray swallowed audibly, gulping as he rubbed his eyes with the back of his hand. "Thanks, Dad. I guess I was stupid not to have trusted you sooner. I should have known that you'd be cool."

I blinked back tears of my own as Corbin reached across the table to catch his son's hand. "It's a scary thing to share personal truths, especially with something like this. I get it, kiddo. I'm not offended, I'm just glad that you finally felt comfortable enough to share." After he pulled his hand away, he casually cut into his enchilada while he asked Gray another question. "I need to know something, son. Is this what all the fights have been about lately? You're not being bullied, are you?"

Gray froze for a few seconds, caught like a deer in the headlights as he stared across the table at his father. He gulped again before nodding. "Yeah, that Clark douche doesn't like it when I wear femme shirts or makeup." He shuddered as he took a breath. "And he's really not gonna like it when I let my hair grow out, I bet."

"*Oh, hell no.* I'll jerk him bald," I snarled, slapping my palm against the table. "Let him touch you again, boo-boo. I don't care how old he is—Miss Kandi will wipe that sucker off the face of the earth. They can arrest me if they want to, but that little shit had better give his heart to Jesus, because his butt is mine." I paused for a moment, then wagged a finger. "Actually, I have a better idea that will keep my happy ass out of the slammer. I'll just loan you the devil dog one day. All that jerk needs to do is meet my gams' not-so-sweet baby Jeebus and he'll be singing a different tune."

Corbin and I both smiled as Gray started laughing so hard that he started hiccupping. Tapping my fingers on the tabletop for a moment, I remembered that I had my own invitation I needed to extend. After Gray had calmed down, I looked back and forth between the two Davis boys. "So, how would you guys feel about me returning your hospitality? I'd like you guys to come to dinner at my place this weekend so you can meet my gam-gam. She's been wanting to meet my boyfriend anyway, and she'll just adore you, Gray. But make sure you douse yourselves with holy water first—I'm not kidding about the satanic dog. He's Beelzebub's minion, I tell you."

Gray tilted his head thoughtfully as he looked at the two of us. "Wow. You guys must be getting kinda serious if you're meeting each other's families. Thanks for inviting me too, Andy. I'd love to come. If nothing else, I think I need to meet this demonic dog. That name is cool though. How did you come up with it?"

I shuddered dramatically. "I know y'all think I'm crazy, but that dog is evil incarnate. As for his name? You'll understand when you hear him sneeze. And trust me, you will hear it because Pekingese dogs snort, snuffle, and sneeze their asses off."

Corbin chuckled as he shook his head. "Just name the time and place, babe. We'll be there—with bells on."

I ignored the babe endearment, tucking it away in the back of my mind to savor later as I dropped my fork with a clatter. "Oh, yeah! That reminds me." I turned sideways in my chair and lifted a foot in the air, pulling my pants up just enough to show off the hand-beaded turquoise anklet with little silver bells. Shaking my foot to make them jingle, I grinned at Corbin. "See? I wasn't lying, boo. I really did come with bells on."

12

CORBIN

After all the questions Gray had asked me about Andy's and my relationship on the drive over, I was feeling pretty guilty as we walked up to his front door. Gray stood beside me, looking curiously around the yard—and the dozens of various lawn gnomes that surrounded it—while I rang the bell.

The sound of a dog going ballistic was clearly audible through the door. Gray and I exchanged a grin when we heard Andy fussing and telling him to hush. When he opened the door, a streak of muddy brown fur came flying out.

"Jeebus! Dagnabbit, get back here! You know you're not allowed out front, you naughty boy." Andy fussed, smiling apologetically at us as he squeezed by in pursuit of the dog. I looked over in the middle of the lawn and almost busted a gut laughing.

The most innocent little face I'd ever seen on a dog stared back at me as he squatted to pee. With his smashed-in looking snout, black face, and what appeared to be only one eye, he was too adorable for words. Gray leaned close enough to whisper in my ear. "That dog doesn't look very satanic to me. He looks like a teddy bear."

Andy snapped his head in our direction. "I heard that, Judas. Trust me, he knows how to look angelic when he wants to, but this dog is evil incarnate. Why won't anyone believe me?" He took a step forward, bending to pick up the dog.

Right as his hands almost closed around the dog's ribs, Jeebus took off like greased lightning—kicking his back paws up and making Andy lose his balance. Andy landed flat on his stomach, face first in the very patch of grass where Jeebus had just taken a piss.

While Andy came up on his hands and knees, sputtering and spitting out grass with a disgusted look on his face, Jeebus ran around him in circles, yapping and wagging his tail. I almost lost it, especially when I glanced to my right and saw Gray holding up his phone and obviously recording the whole fiasco. I lifted a brow and he just shrugged as if to say *what?*

Andy pushed to his feet, running around like a hunchbacked caveman from a B-grade movie as he scrambled around the grass trying to get the dog who easily eluded him at every turn. I squatted on the front step and snapped my fingers. "Jeebus. Come here, boy," I called in a firm tone that brooked no argument.

Jeebus froze mid-step, one paw in the air as he tilted his head to peer at me with his single eye. I snapped my fingers again, repeating the command. Jeebus sneezed loudly, the sound nearly an exact match for his name —*jeee-buss!*—then wagged his tail and ran right over, stopping in front of me with his front paws pushed together and his back end up in the air wiggling excitedly as if he were presenting himself for inspection.

"Good boy," I commended him as I scooped him up against my chest and stood. I glanced at Gray. "Did you hear that adorable sneeze? I guess we know how he got his name now."

"Jesus, Mary, and Joseph, y'all need to hold on for a darn minute. Did that little shit seriously just come when you called him?" Andy stood aghast, glaring at the dog with his hands on his hips as he took in the scene. His head whipped in Gray's direction. "Et tu, brute? You're seriously recording this bullshit? Actually, never mind... I'm glad you did, so thank you for that. Hell, put it on YouTube. Maybe there will be at least one impartial witness who will view it and agree that this dog is pure evil."

Gray and I both bit back laughs as Andy huffed and walked toward us, mumbling under his breath with every step. He paused when he got onto the stoop, reaching up to scratch Jeebus behind the ears—an affectionate move that belied everything he'd ever said about the pooch. "If you ever make me land face first in a puddle of your piss again, Imma tie a knot in your tail, Beelzebub." Jeebus chuffed as though he found the threat humorous. Gray and I were both smart enough to keep our mouths shut and our expressions neutral as we followed Andy inside.

I waited until the door was shut to set Jeebus down, but he didn't go far. He seemed content to sniff my shoes and pant legs. The room was dimly lit, and I had to blink a few times before my eyes adjusted. My mouth fell open when I noticed a familiar face sitting in a faded recliner across the room. Before Andy could introduce us, I started to chuckle as I recognized one of my worst, most cantankerous patients whose spunk I secretly adored. "Miss Loretta? Of all the gin joints, in all the world... do you mean to tell me that *you're* Andy's famous gam-gam?"

"Oh, hell." She shot me a dirty look before turning a mutinous face toward Andy. "Are you kidding me with this one, princess? You're dating Dr. Pain in the Ass? No, this needs to end now. I do not approve."

I gulped as I turned to Andy. But he was simply standing there, his arms crossed over his chest as he leaned on one hip, tapping his foot impatiently. "Nope. Sorry. You don't get to make that call, old lady. Especially when your barking dust mop just shoved my face in his piss out there."

Loretta wheezed as she cackled. "He didn't! My sweet boy

wouldn't ever do something like that. Quit lying about your fuzzy uncle."

"Ask the kid here, he's got the damning proof on his phone since he filmed the whole blessed thing," Andy said, a single brow quirked as he glared somewhat playfully at his grandmother. "Now tell me what problem you could possibly have with my hot-as-fuck boyfriend." He swallowed and shot Gray an apologetic smile. "Oops. Forget I said that about your dad. That shit ain't right." Gray just laughed and squatted to pet Jeebus, who was pawing at my pant legs and trying to get my attention.

Loretta glared in my direction. "Dr. Pain in the Ass here is the reason I had to quit smoking. He's one of those damned nicotine Nazis who wants to steal away smokers' rights and police them into his way of thinking."

Andy rolled his eyes. "You mean he made you quit smoking openly. Are you forgetting that I busted you with those sneaky shitter cigs? Cuz they count, old woman."

I choked at the scandalized look on Loretta's face, trying my best not to laugh. "Miss Loretta, have you been sneaking cigarettes in the bathroom? You know what I told you about smoking."

She turned to Andy and shook a gnarled fist. "Snitches get stitches, you little narc."

Andy laughed as he rushed over and bussed her cheek. "Oh, hush. You know you love me. You just don't like being caught."

Loretta's face screwed up as she shied away from him. "Good gawd almighty, what the hell is that smell coming off your face, princess?"

He kissed her again, laughing as she swatted at him while he danced back with a triumphant smirk. "That lovely aroma would the scent of that aforementioned piss your precious angel baby *didn't* make me fall in."

She gagged and held up her hands. "Help me up, brat. We both need to wash our faces before dinner. Honestly, you really should've said something and excused yourself to wash up the minute you came in. I thought you were just talking trash about my sweet boy again. How the hell was I supposed to know you were serious this time?"

Andy rolled his eyes as he went to help her up. "Yeah, because I really make up all the ways that dog tries to fuck with me."

Loretta waited until she was steady on her feet before smacking him upside the head. "Watch your mouth, princess. We don't speak French in this house. I've let it slide too many times today; don't make me wash your mouth out with soap."

I looked down at Gray while Andy escorted his grandmother out of the room, smiling to see him grinning, seemingly as charmed by the two of them as I was while they bickered their way down the hall.

By the time we finished dinner—or supper, as they called it —an hour later, Loretta and I had become fast friends.

Mostly because Jeebus had decided he was in love with me, and apparently anyone he adored was aces in her book. The dog had sat between us at the small, round table throughout the entire meal. He hadn't begged or gotten underfoot, he'd just sat panting happily at his two favorite people.

Andy sent us into the living room to relax after dinner while he finished cleaning up. I was proud to see Gray insist on helping while I escorted Loretta back to her chair. I took a seat on the couch across from her, unsurprised to see Jeebus jump up beside me. "Is he allowed on the furniture?" I asked, my hand already poised midair, ready to pet him.

"That's fine, sweetheart. My baby boy is allowed to get on anything he wants in this house; it's his home too, isn't it?" Loretta smiled fondly at her beloved Pekingese while I stroked his long, fluffy fur. She watched us for a few minutes before smiling at me as a cagey look came into her eyes. "So, Dr. Pain in the Ass, I believe this is the point where I ask what your intentions are toward my grandson. Although I am glad to see that you're good for something. You've obviously raised a fine young man there, and you seem to make both my grandson and my sweet baby happy."

"What are you on about now, old woman?" Andy asked as he came into the room with Gray right behind him. Jeebus jumped onto my lap, as if to claim me, when Andy sat down on the couch. Shooting the dog a dirty look, he scooted closer until we were sitting snug up against each other, hip to hip. Wagging a finger in Jeebus' face, Andy spoke in a voice filled with sugary-sweet baby talk. "Snuggle on up to him, you little monster. But just remember, he was mine first and I'm only sharing because I'm nice."

Jeebus stood on his hind legs, balancing on each of my thighs and resting his front paws against my chest as he licked under my chin. Loretta chuckled. "I think my baby might beg to differ, brat. He's laying claim to your man. Just look at how happy he is, the little sweetie pie." She looked up at Gray, who was standing awkwardly as if unsure of himself, and patted the chair beside her. "Come over here and sit a spell, young man. I don't bite... much."

While Gray did as she'd told him, Andy rested his head on my shoulder—which I had to admit, I didn't hate. He made kissing noises at Jeebus, who was still busily licking my chin. "Why can't you love me like that, you little brat? I wouldn't call you a devil dog if you'd ever show me this angelic side. Remember, I *am* the one who feeds you."

Jeebus leaned over and licked Andy's cheek, then went back to work on my chin. Andy pulled back with a gasp, holding a palm to his cheek as he stared at the little dog in shock. "Did you guys see that? He kissed my cheek! I think he's decided to like me now. Maybe because I brought Corbin into his life. Who knows why, but I'll take it." He rested his cheek against my shoulder again and cooed at the dog. "I guess even a devil dog can find salvation. But if we're going to be friends now, you'll need to remember one pertinent fact—Corbin is still my boyfriend, not yours, little dog."

Jeebus leaned over as if to lick him again, only to bite Andy's cheek. Andy jerked back, jumping up from the couch with a loud shriek and jumping from foot to foot like he was putting out a fire as he spun around in a circle. "I've been maimed! Dear God, somebody call an ambulance because I've probably got rabies. No, my gawd! I bet it's even worse—holy hell, I bet I'm about to be possessed by Satan's right-hand man! Somebody call a priest, quick! Tell him to bring a gallon of holy water and at least three strands of rosary beads. And make sure he's not some junior priest either, we're gonna need to bring in the big guns on this one."

Loretta was giggling so hard, I was pretty sure she may have peed a little, and as for me, I was laughing way too much to do anything to help poor Andy. Gray was the one who came to his aid. He tried several times before he finally managed to grab Andy's shoulders long enough to get him to be still. "Hold on, man. Let me look." He peered closely at Andy's cheek, then shook his head. "There's not even a mark, dude. Seriously, are you sure he even bit you?"

Andy stopped, visibly calming down as he rubbed his cheek and glared at Jeebus. "The only reason there's not a mark is because he probably doesn't have any teeth left, aside from maybe a nub or two. *Still*. Keep an eye on me, okay? If I start speaking Latin backwards, I need you to promise to call a priest. Don't let me get to the point where my head's doing a three-sixty and I'm puking green goo before you get someone with a cross on the case, you hear me?"

Gray stared calmly back at Andy. "Do you even speak Latin? Because I don't, so how will I know if that's even what you're speaking?"

When Andy looked completely speechless for probably the first time in his life, I found myself laughing all over again. Damn, but if I wasn't completely charmed by the guy.

13

ANDY

"I hate to break it to you, darlin'. If you're still hot and heavy with your fake man after three weeks, then maybe things aren't quite as pretend as you both seem to think." Mama Honey leaned over my shoulder to see who I was texting.

Holding up the phone, I smiled helplessly. "I'm texting with Gray right now, not Corbin. How am I supposed to shut things down when I've got such a connection going with his son? He's a cute baby enby who's just trying to find his wings. I can't abandon him now, that would just be ugly of me."

Honey walked back over to her own table, dropping heavily onto her stool as she shook her head. "Lord have mercy, it's worse than I thought. If you've bonded with his son, then I'm afraid that I don't see an end game here. How are you guys supposed to have a fake breakup when you're friends with his teenage son? Honestly, gurl. You didn't think this one through, did you?"

"Probably not," I admitted with a rueful smile. "The two of them were so lost, Honey. You should've seen them, it would've broken your heart. Both of them were simply longing to talk to each other, but neither one thought the other wanted to listen. It was as obvious as the nose on my face once I got to know them."

Honey sighed heavily. "And how are things between you and baby enby's daddy dearest? Have you kissed him yet? Or are you at least keeping things smart in that department?" She chuckled, shaking her head. "Listen to me, advising you not to kiss that sexy hunk of man. Hell, we both know that I'd be kissing him every chance I could get—and I'm not talking about on his lips, either. Dammit, baby girl. The way you guys are headed, you're either gonna be stuck in the friend zone with no way out, or married to the man by Christmas."

"Pshaw, that won't happen. You know my rule. I'd never marry anyone without being courted for a minimum of a year. That's too big of a life decision to make with someone you haven't spent at least four seasons with—that's just common sense right there."

"You say that now, but just wait until you finally meet that magical peen. Those things have a way of making us do things we never thought we'd do—and if we're lucky, maybe a few we've secretly fantasized about, if you get my drift." Honey's deep, bawdy laugh made me grin.

My phone alerted me of a new text, but I waited until I'd affixed my false lashes before looking at the message. I did a mental happy dance but tried not to let my excitement show on my face as I turned to Honey. "Corbin's coming to see the show tonight. He's recording my act for Gray. He just texted to see if that was okay, isn't that sweet?"

"Yasss, queen," Honey said with an eye roll. "But don't think I didn't notice you bouncing in your seat there, gurl. If this is you not getting attached, I'd hate to see what you falling in love would entail. My heart can't handle that shit."

"Sorry, Honey. That dog won't hunt—you and I both know that you're lying your ass off because you'd love nothing better than to watch me get twitterpated and partnered up with the boy of my dreams." I reached for my wig, this time a long, straight-haired one that would give me the look of an older, sexier Britney.

"Fine, you got me there," Honey reluctantly admitted. "I just don't want to see you guys lie to yourselves and end up stuck in something that isn't going anywhere. If you want me to get off your ass, then you need to see if you can talk your hot doc into taking you on a real date. If he's as interested in you as I think he is, I don't think he'd turn you down. Either way, at least you'd know where you stand."

I thought about that for a second. As always, my drag mama had made a good point. It wasn't like I hadn't already wanted to go out with Corbin, and hadn't I caught him checking me out more than once? I dropped my chin to my chest in defeat. "But what if he *does* say no, Mama? At least right now, I can pretend he's mine and I'm free to flirt with him anytime I want."

Mama Honey shook her head. "No, baby gurl. That may be nice for a few weeks, but eventually it's going to be as unsatisfying as fat-free cookies or low-sodium potato chips. Like my man Marvin Gaye sang: *Ain't nothing like the real thing, baby.*"

Her words stuck with me for the rest of the night. I was dancing to the final song of my set, "Hit Me Baby One More Time," when I realized just how true the lyrics were as I lip-synched along with the part about my loneliness killing me now. I saw Corbin watching me with what looked like adoration on his face while he held up his phone to record the act for Gray. I somehow found the nerve to blow a kiss right in his direction as I popped my hips to the side and slid my hand slowly along my torso while I sang the words at the end of the stanza.

Give me a sign... hit me baby one more time.

After my act, I was floating on air as I weaved through the crowd, collecting tips and flirting with the customers as I slowly made my way toward the bar where Corbin sat watching me with a secret smile while he chatted with St. Nick. By the time I got there, my white leather bra was stuffed with bills and I was sweating like a pig—or perspiring like an overworked queen, I should say. I nodded a hello to St. Nick and purposefully stepped between Corbin's knees, leaning in to press a loud, smacking kiss onto his cheek. I smiled almost possessively at the perfect lipstick print I'd left when I leaned back to examine his face.

"Why don't you just piss on his leg if you want to mark him as yours, Kandi? It would serve the same purpose, but the smell would probably last a hell of a lot longer," Nick said with a chuckle as he held out a napkin to Corbin to wipe his face.

That damn butterfly fluttered in my stomach again when Corbin shook his head and waved the napkin away. "That's okay, Nick. I'm proud to wear Kandi's brand." When I started to step away, he gripped my hips and pulled me closer. "Where are you trying to get off to so fast, babe? You've branded me, now you have to stick around so people will know where it came from."

His hands slid around to cup my butt, settling almost possessively on the curve of my ass as he linked his fingers together. I wasn't sure how to deal with this, since PTL night was outside of our fake relationship, with Gams and Gray unlikely to hear about this public display of affection.

Deciding I didn't care why he was doing it, I embraced the moment and lifted a brow, loosely wrapping my arms around his neck. I ran my fingers through his hair, scratching his scalp with my press-on nails as I leaned against his chest. "My lands, Kandi could get used to this kind of action," I said in a breathy voice. We stared into each other's eyes for a long moment until I decided to throw caution completely to the wind and leaned in for a kiss. I was a few scant inches from my target when a deep-throated chuckle sounded from directly behind me.

"Well, now. What do we have here? Aren't you going to introduce me, darlin'?" I glanced back over my shoulder to see my drag mother standing there with a wickedly amused smile on her face. When I narrowed my eyes, she held up her hands. "Sorry if I'm cock-blocking what looked like was about to be a pretty hot smooch, but I need a hand, baby gurl. There's been a slight wardrobe malfunction, and Honey isn't ready to go home for the night just yet. Can I pull you in the back for a moment? It won't take long, just two shakes of a lamb's tail, as they say. I'd handle it myself, but I think maybe this is gonna be a two-person tape job."

Corbin released his hold on me as I turned all the way around to look at Honey. I leaned back against my man's chest, resting my hands on his knees as I lifted a brow and gave Mama Honey the once-over. "You don't look like you need help, Mama. But as long as you're here, let me introduce you to my man. This is Corbin." I looked over my shoulder with a smile. "I'd like you to meet my drag mother, boo—this is the fabulous Miss Honey Combover, who's going to be on her way now because she was just making up an excuse to meet you."

"All right, you asked for it, darlin'." Honey gave a weary sigh as if I were the one putting her out. I almost choked when she simply turned and lifted her leg to plant her size fifteen stiletto on the rung of the bar stool beside us, cocking out a hip to show me that there was indeed a problem.

As she bent forward over the stool, her too-short skirt slowly lifted higher until we were greeted by the sight of a big, hairy ass in all its glory. Why she'd chosen to wear a thong was beyond me, but her tape had somehow gotten twisted in the string and a long, thick uncut cock and furry sac dangled below the hem of her micro-mini. I almost kept my laughter inside, and likely would have succeeded, until Honey decided she needed to twerk. Every move made that schlong sway to and fro, banging against her sac with every move and curling back around it as if to say hello.

"Stop, I can't take anymore!" I managed to get out between bursts of laughter. "Damn, Honey. I swear that thing looks like a snake swinging from a tree branch. I think it's looking for something—or someone—to eat."

Honey stopped her dance and turned around, easing onto the stool and leaning against the bar with a triumphant smile. The snake peeked out at us from beneath her skirt, resting on the edge of the seat, poking its fool head out as if looking for air. "See? I told you I'd had a malfunction, but noooo... you just wouldn't listen. And yes, my poor snake is quite hungry, now that you mention it." Honey waggled her eyebrows, running her pink tongue over shiny ruby-red lips. "Actually, I think the poor thing's on life support. Maybe a little mouth-to-tip resuscitation is in order." Tapping her fingers on the bar, she peered around me to catch Corbin's eye. "You're a doctor, aren't you, darlin'? Maybe you'd have the sort of medical knowledge to assist in that regard?"

I reached back behind my head to cover Corbin's mouth before he could answer, while wagging the pointer finger of my free hand at Honey. "Take your ass on and find your own medical professional, this one's taken." And just because she'd decided to put the flirt on with my man— fake or not—I decided to get a little sassy with her. "And Honey, maybe the real problem is that you ought not wear micro-minis when your dangly bits are that large and in charge. Either that or find some tape with a little more staying power, just sayin'."

Honey threw her head back with a laugh as she stood from the stool and leaned in to kiss my cheek. "Keep telling yourself it's fake with Dr. Hottie, darlin'. Say it enough times, and maybe you'll believe it," she whispered in my ear before turning and wiggling her fingers with a flirty goodbye to Corbin as she sashayed away, that snake swinging back to peek out under the edge of her skirt, as if waving its own farewell.

14

CORBIN

Dana nearly fell out of her chair laughing when I told her the story of the fabulously bearded Mama Honey and her swinging cock-snake the next morning. We were having a cup of coffee after the kids had gone to school while I showed her the footage from Kandi's routine.

"Seriously, Dana. You really need to come with me one of these weeks. The kids are old enough to stay home alone, and you deserve a night out. You wouldn't believe how much fun it is down there. And Andy, when he's in his Kandi persona? Damn, she's just dynamite. Honestly, it's like I'm seeing two separate people who share one body."

Her teacup clattered against the saucer as Dana stared at me. "You like him, don't you? You really do. Oh, Corb. That's the best news I've had in months. I like seeing you smile, and if Andy is the one putting it on your face, then I'm on board."

I felt my cheeks heat as I blushed. I took a quick drink of coffee to settle myself before responding. "Well, sure, I like him. I'm dating him, aren't I? He's a great guy. And he's been instrumental in helping me connect better with Gray. The two of them are thick as thieves now; I catch Gray texting him all the time."

Dana rolled her eyes. "Spare me, please. I don't need whatever bullshit line you think I need to hear, just be honest with me. You actually like your fake boyfriend, don't you?"

My eyes bugged out as I stared at her in shock. "You figured me out, huh? I should've known that I couldn't pull a fast one on you."

"Sweetie, you'd have to get up pretty early in the morning to pull one on me. How long have we known each other? Please. As if you'd ever be cool enough to have a secret boyfriend that you didn't tell your best friend about. Damn straight I knew, and from the moment Becca told me, too. I haven't bugged you about it because I figured you'd open up in your own time. But since that hasn't happened, now it's time for me to pry. Now tell me all about him. From what I've heard, I already know I'm a fan."

I slouched down in my chair, crossing my arms over my chest as I allowed myself to relax. "He's just so damn adorable. He's loyal as hell, and always there to help anyone who needs it. His entire life is pretty much spent either working or taking care of his grandmother. The one thing he allows himself is his Thursday nights at Saint's

Place." I smiled as I pictured Andy, trying to figure out where to begin describing him. "He's got like five different smiles that I know of so far. My favorite is when he's being fake and he does this cute little nose scrunch for that smile."

"Man, you do have it bad. Tell me more," Dana demanded as she lifted her cup for another sip of tea.

"What do you want to know? Hair color, eye color? Age and political affiliations? I mean, I'm not sure where we're going here." I stopped for a moment as I pictured his face. "But speaking of his eyes, those are pretty unique. I thought they were green at first, but they change colors and I don't know if it's because of what he's wearing, his mood, or what—but I'd kinda like to find out. They're hazel with green and gold flecks in them, but then sometimes they're green with hints of gold and brown. It's like, I don't know what color they are, you know? Are they brown? Are they green? Are they some sort of optical mood ring that would clue me into his emotions? I feel like I should know this, but I don't."

"Corb, you do realize that you're ridiculous, right?" Dana shook her head, her eyes crinkling with amusement. "Have you ever thought of asking him? Or hell, ask one of your doctor friends. You've got to know an optician or an ophthalmologist, right?"

"I can't just ask him something like that. It's not like we're really dating, although maybe we should be at this point." As soon as I said it, the truth of that statement hit me. I looked back at Dana with surprise. "Holy shit, I should ask him out, shouldn't I? Wait, would that be weird? Are you allowed to ask somebody you're fake dating out for real?"

"You're lucky I'm the parent of a teenage girl, and therefore equipped to have followed that sentence. But as for asking him out? I don't see why you couldn't. Honestly, I don't see why you didn't just ask him out in the first place. It's obvious that you thought he was cute, and it's not like you weren't both single. I think this whole fake relationship was just an excuse for both of you to get closer to each other without putting yourselves out there. Grow a pair, sweetie. Ask him out." Before I could talk myself out of it, I snatched up my phone and shot off a text.

Hey, how would you feel about going on a real date with your fake boyfriend?

Dana grabbed my phone to see what I'd sent then passed it back and held her hand up for a high five. I'd barely pulled my hand back when my phone pinged.

New phone, who dis? LOL, just kidding. That depends. Are you asking how I'd feel or asking for a date? Sorry, boo. The intent of your message wasn't clear. Better try again.

I grinned as I read his text and sent back my response.

I'm asking for a date, babe. So what do you say? Do you want to go out with me?

After a few seconds, Dana scooted her chair around so she could follow along with the conversation. I leaned off to the side with a playful pout. "What do you think you're doing, nosy?"

Dana rolled her eyes. "Duh. I'm obviously being nosy, as you've already said. That's not a secret. Now get back over here so I can see the screen too." We both grinned as the next message came in.

I mean, I was planning to wash my hair Friday night. I could be talked out of it, I suppose. Name the time and place, boo. Tracy's leaning over my shoulder and frothing at the mouth. We need details.

"You know what I like about this guy? He doesn't use text speak. He types complete sentences and doesn't skimp on punctuation. I respect that," Dana commented as she read the message.

My fingers hovered over the keyboard. "Where should I take him? That new seafood place downtown, maybe? Or then again, there's always Flanagan's. You can't go wrong with a good pub, right?"

Dana thought about that for a moment, then shook her head. "Pass me your phone, I know just what to say."

"Screw that, I don't need my own personal Cyrano de Bergerac. I can handle talking to my fake boyfriend, thank you very much." I rolled my eyes and began typing.

I hear you about Tracy. My friend Dana's frothing at the bit over my shoulder too. How about this? We start off with a walk around the downtown area and see where the evening takes us.

"Ooh, nicely played, Dr. Davis. That way you have a chance to talk, spend a little time together without feeling rushed by someone bugging you every few minutes to ask how everything is... yes, I approve. That's a good plan." Dana bumped her shoulder against mine. "I hope you know I'll need a play-by-play afterward, right?"

Before I could answer, Andy's reply came through.

That sounds like perfection. Plus, I won't feel guilty if I overindulge because we will have gotten in a little exercise beforehand. Tracy says to tell you that she approves too.

I chuckled and sent back a quick message.

The idea got Dana's stamp of approval as well. Pick you up at six?

The phone pinged almost immediately.

Fabulous. Now tell Dana goodbye and get your ass to work, I haven't seen my favorite customer yet today.

Dana chuckled as I set the phone down. "You guys are too cute for words. This is going to be so much fun to watch."

"Where is Gray tonight, at his friend's house?" Andy and I had been walking through downtown as planned, looking into shop windows and casually chatting as we got to know each other better.

"He will be later; right now he's at a school dance with Becca. He doesn't usually go to them, but she talked him into it." I shook my head. "It's hard not to be a helicopter parent, but I hope things go well tonight. He wore a short, pink dress like a long shirt with skinny jeans and topped it with one of his mom's old belts he dug up from somewhere. And before you ask, his shoes were Doc Martens. He even had a little makeup on." I took a breath. "It's so hard, you know? It's like, I want him to be free to be himself, but I'm worried about him getting bullied. But he should be fine, right? And Dana is chaperoning, so she'll be there to keep an eye on him. Damn, you should've seen him, Andy. He looked cute, and more importantly, he actually seemed happy and comfortable in his own skin. His hair is growing out enough that it curls around his ears, have you noticed?"

Andy nodded. "Yeah, he sent me a picture of a hairstyle he wants to try. He wants to shave the right side of his head, just a few inches over the ear all the way across from front to back, dye it pink, then let the rest of it grow and stay brown so he can style it with different colored gels if he wants. Don't be surprised when he brings it up to you; the only reason he hasn't is because he's not sure about it yet. I think he was using me as a sounding board for fashion advice, so don't feel left out."

"No, not at all," I said, turning to flash him a quick smile to let him know that I wasn't concerned. "I'm not exactly a guy someone would look to for fashion advice, let alone tips on hair and makeup. I'm just glad he turns to you. He needs that connection he's found with you."

"Happy to do it. Gray's a great kid," Andy said easily. His smile looked a little brittle as he shook his head. "He's fortunate to have a parent who is willing to let him express himself and be whoever he wants to be."

I pointed to a bench just up ahead. "Feel like taking a break?" When Andy nodded his agreement, I led him over and took a seat. As he settled in beside me, I rested my arm over the back, letting my hand land on his shoulder and lightly holding him against me. "Why do I have a feeling that you were speaking from experience just now? How did you come to live with your grandmother anyway? I've never heard you speak about your own family."

Andy huffed out a breath. "Yeah, I suppose it is about time for that conversation, isn't it? Gams is my only family now —my own disowned me when I turned eighteen. Gams doesn't talk to her own son anymore, after he kicked me out. It was my birthday, and we were all out at a restaurant. The waiter was super cute, and my dad frowned when he was flirting with me. After he walked away, my dad made a homophobic comment that should've clued me in. But see, I'd had this big plan that I was going to come out to my family on my birthday. I thought it would be memorable. And boy was it, just maybe not in the way that I'd planned for it to be. When we got home, my dad gave me long enough to pack whatever I could fit into my suitcase before showing me the door. My mom and sister just sat there and watched it happen. Their parting words were that they'd pray for me."

Hugging him closer, I rested my cheek on the top of his head. "I'm sorry, Andy. That's so unfair. I've never understood how parents could turn their backs on their own children just because they don't agree with who they are. Don't those people realize that sexuality isn't a choice? We like what we like, that's just how life is. That's like saying people who hate artichokes are choosing not to like them, just because they prefer brussels sprouts."

Andy laughed into my shoulder. "Good one. Well, can I just say that you're one of the nicest brussels sprouts I've come across so far? I know you like both artichokes and brussels sprouts, and that's okay too. How did that fly with your parents?"

"I'm almost embarrassed to admit this after hearing your story, but my parents were totally cool with it. They didn't care who I dated, as long as they treated me well and I was equally respectful. All my folks ever wanted was for me to be happy. That's what I want to give Gray, the same unconditional love and support that I had with my parents."

"You mention your parents in the past tense. Are they gone now, or do they just live far away?" Andy spoke carefully, as if already knowing the answer.

HOW NOT TO BLEND

"Wow, we really are getting to the tough questions tonight, aren't we? Next you'll be asking me about my dead wife." I blew out a breath, chuckling as I ran the backs of my fingers over his arm. "Yeah, my parents passed away a few years before Maria. I was one of those change-of-life surprise babies. Mom was nearly fifty when I was born, and Dad was eight years older. I was just happy that they both lived long enough to see their grandson be born. And also that they both passed before Maria, because watching her die would've broken their hearts. I like to think that they're all together now."

Andy tilted his head back to make eye contact, his hand coming up to rest on my chest. "It sounds like we've both had our fair share of pain. And I want you to know that you don't ever have to tell me about Maria, if you're not comfortable talking about it."

I smiled as I reached up to brush the hair out of his eyes where the wind had blown it in his face. "It's okay. We weren't even supposed to have ended up together, to be honest. We were seniors in college and had plans to go our own ways after graduation. But then she got pregnant and we got married. You know how it goes. We may not have been the loves of each other's lives, but we cared about each other. And the longer we were together, the closer we got. Dana was her college roommate. She's the reason we settled here in Rockford Bluff."

Andy smiled. "That explains why you're so tight. That's good that you were there for each other after you both lost

Maria. The fact that your kids are also best friends is super sweet, and an added layer of connection, I bet. I'm glad you've had each other. Did Maria have a long struggle with her cancer?"

"No, not at all." I sighed, hating to remember those days, but needing to share. "The cancer was too far along by the time it was diagnosed. You hear of people struggling for years and dying these long, horrible deaths, but that wasn't Maria. And I'm very grateful for that, by the way. We barely had three months from diagnosis until we lost her. They were a good three months because she lived every day as though it were her last and did her best to make as many solid memories with Gray as she could. It was a horrible experience, and I'll always miss her, but I'm grateful that she didn't suffer. And as selfish as this will sound, I'm equally grateful that Gray and I didn't have to watch her suffer."

Andy looked down again, resting his head against my chest as he spoke in a voice so soft I almost had to strain to hear it. "I don't know how you survived it. When I almost lost Gams last summer, it was the worst moment of my life. I know I don't have that much time left with her, and I'm constantly afraid that I'm going to lose her. Her heart gave out so fast last time, we didn't have any warning. I don't know if it's better that I know it's coming this time, or if I'd rather have been blissfully unaware of the Grim Reaper waiting in the wings."

"You can't think like that, babe." I winced as the fake

endearment spilled out of my lips so naturally, and quickly rushed to cover my faux pas. "Your grandmother is much healthier than she was last summer. Not to brag, but I've heard that she's being seen by a top-notch cardiologist." I chuckled then continued. "Don't worry, Andy. I'm keeping a close eye on Loretta. I'll do everything I can to help keep that Grim Reaper at bay for as long as possible."

"I mean, she is eighty-three years old. Logically, I know that she's had a good run and won't live forever. But I'm just not ready to lose her yet, you know?" Andy pulled away, sitting up to get his phone out. He held it up to show me. "It's after eight o'clock; we've been walking and talking for so long that we've made it past the dinner rush. Ready to find some food? I don't know about you, but I'm starving."

"That sounds like a plan," I said, then laughed when my stomach decided to growl right then. "And apparently, my gut agrees."

When I stood to join him, I caught his hand in mine as we headed back toward a small Italian bistro we'd passed earlier and had already agreed we'd go back to for dinner. As he started to take a step forward, I yanked on our joined hands and decided to take a chance, twirling him back against me as though we were dancing. He laughed when he bumped up against me, his back to my chest. When he looked up to say something, I caught his chin with my free hand and held his face with a loose grip. "I'm going to kiss you now, Andy. If you don't want it, now's your chance to say something."

Andy's only response was to snake his hand around the back of my head and pull me closer. Our lips met for a soft kiss that neither of us let linger too long. We both pulled back, gazing into each other's eyes with what felt like wonder. "Your lips are moist. I like the way they feel," I blurted randomly.

I blushed when he started laughing, twirling himself back around and tugging me with our joined hands to walk toward the restaurant. Once Andy quit laughing, he grinned up at me. "It's called lip gloss, that's what makes them moist. And by the way? You're pretty damn cute when you blush, Dr. Hottie."

We talked and laughed like old friends all the way to the restaurant, and even though it was a Friday night, the place had cleared out enough that we were easily able to get a table. We'd barely made it through the appetizers when my phone went off. I started to ignore it, but Andy shook his head. "Go ahead, you're a parent first, I get that. Make sure it's not something important."

Pulling out my phone, I flashed him a grateful smile that froze in place the minute I read the message on my screen from Dana.

Emergency! Gray was taken by ambulance to the ER. Get there as fast as you can, he wasn't conscious.

Unable to speak, I held the phone up for Andy to read. He

immediately pointed toward the door. "Go, get out of here. I'll catch the bill and handle things here. Your car is parked less than a block away."

With a quick nod, I jumped from my seat and started to rush away when I remembered that I'd picked Andy up. I was halfway back to the table when he shook his head, waving me off. "I'll be fine, I meant it when I said I've got this. I'll just call myself an Uber. You go to Gray. Just promise you'll call if you need me? I don't care how late it is, I'll be there if you want me."

I nodded quickly, taking a deep breath as I turned and sprinted through the restaurant. I was just pushing the doors open to leave when I realized that I didn't want to do this alone, and I also didn't want to make Andy feel like he wasn't wanted.

Andy looked up in shock when I ran back up to the table. I pulled out my wallet and dropped a hundred-dollar bill on the table and reached for Andy's hand. "This is me calling you because I need you. Please come with me; I didn't mean to almost shut you out. Honestly, I could really use a friend right now."

As Andy and I raced together toward my car, it occurred to me that I'd already have a friend waiting at the hospital in Dana. But that wouldn't have been enough. I needed Andy there too, and didn't really care what that meant. Right now, the only thing that mattered was getting to Gray—with Andy at my side.

Several hours later, Gray had been moved to a private room and admitted after briefly regaining consciousness. He'd been worked over pretty badly, but thankfully no bones had been broken and he wasn't showing signs of internal bleeding. The only worry now was whether he had a concussion, which I was pretty sure he did, and whether he'd suffered any brain trauma from the attack. The tests had come back clear, so now it was just a matter of letting him rest until his body was ready to wake up.

Andy and Dana followed me out of Gray's hospital room where we'd left Becca to sit with him while we took a break. I needed to get out of there and find some air where I didn't have to see my son hooked up to machines before I lost my mind. Neither one of them commented when I kicked a chair across the empty waiting room we found ourselves in. Andy went to retrieve the chair and put it back in place while Dana caught me by the shoulders and got up in my face. "He's going to be okay, Corb. That's the important part. I know you're upset—so am I—but you've got to hold it together, sweetie. Right now isn't the time to lose your shit."

"Fuck that, Dana. Tell me if that was Becca in there that you wouldn't be reacting the same damn way. My son is lying in that room hooked up to machines after being beaten to the point of losing consciousness. And why? Because he dared to wear something pink and lacy to a fucking dance! No, Dana, I'm not upset. Upset is when he gets a bad grade or I find a false charge on my credit card bill. This is me being fucking livid." I shoved away from her, walking over to where Andy sat quietly off to the side. I dropped into a chair beside him and absently reached for his hand. I calmed down a little at his touch and waited a few minutes before I spoke again. "I don't care how this sounds, but I just want to find that Danvers kid and shove my fist down his throat."

"You're allowed to be as angry as you need to be, Corbin. Get it out now so that you can pull it together when Gray's awake again. Trust me, if that bully's ass was here right now, I'd help you take him down. You just let it out, and do whatever you need to do. Punch a wall, throw the furniture around, rage scream if you must... just let it out." I didn't know why, but Andy was able to reach me and soothe me in ways that Dana couldn't. I clung to his hand, rubbing my thumb across the back of his knuckles as I sat there quietly fuming.

I felt eyes on me and glanced up to see Dana looking at our joined hands, but keeping whatever thoughts she may have had to herself for the moment. At any other time or place, she probably would've been teasing me. When I met her eyes, she smiled gently as if to let me know that she understood.

Dana came over and sat down beside me a few minutes later, reaching for my other hand. "I'm so sorry, Corb. I know you were counting on me to watch him, but he was in the boys' bathroom when it happened. It was the one place I couldn't go. And as for Clark Danvers, there were no witnesses to the assault. Until Gray wakes up and tells us who did it, no charges can be pressed. We're just lucky that he was found quickly."

Andy practically growled. "So basically, what you're telling us is that Gray went to take a leak and got jumped? That is not okay. And as for the no witnesses thing, there's got to be documented stuff on file of that punk and Gray getting into fights, right? Shouldn't that be enough for them to at least question the kid?"

I rolled my head back to look up at the ceiling as I blew out a breath. "Damn, I really wish I could punch something right now. But no, that's not enough for them to question the Danvers kid. As far as the school is concerned, their fights were mutual. They don't have it recorded as Gray being bullied. If he and Becca hadn't told us, we wouldn't even have known that ourselves."

Before our conversation could go any further, one of the nurses came in the room. "Dr. Davis? Your son is waking up."

15

ANDY

The following afternoon, I was keeping Gray company in his room while Corbin went downstairs to get some lunch. Gray looked at me with a frown. "How long did they say I have to stay here again? I just want to go home and curl up in my own bed."

Shaking my head, I moved to the foot of his bed and sat down beside him. "I know, boo-boo. Nothing sucks worse than being in the hospital, I can't argue with that. But you've got a concussion and they needed to keep you for observation. I wouldn't be surprised if you got to go home in the morning. Hell, if you were an adult, they'd probably have kicked you to the curb by now. But they have to be more careful with minors."

"The doctor said that the police want to talk to me. Is Dad going to make me answer their questions?" He turned his head to look out the window, discreetly wiping away a stray tear. "I'd rather not, if I don't have to. Can't we just forget it happened?"

I breathed heavily as I took his hand and held it in mine. "It doesn't work that way, boo-boo. You need to tell them who did it, because they don't need to get away with assault and battery. If they got away with it this time, who knows what would happen the next time around? Maybe not to you, but eventually there'd be another victim, and probably another after that until they finally get their ass caught. And we both know how bad you'd feel if that happened when you could have prevented it."

Gray sniffled, rubbing the back of his hand across his eyes. "You don't understand, if I tell then he will kill me next time. He said if I talked then I'd be dead."

"Oh, honey." I leaned forward and gave him a gentle hug before sitting back to talk some more. "Bullying assholes always say that shit, because they don't want to get caught. Listen, when I was in high school, one of my friends had something like this happen. She was a lesbian and tried to keep to herself. She was just trying to survive like everyone else, you know how it is at your age. Well, there was this group of bitchy cheerleaders that had it out for her. They did all sorts of ugly shit to that girl. And even though she never talked, it just escalated until she wasn't talking to anyone, even me."

"Did she finally tell?" Gray spoke hesitantly, as if afraid to hear the answer.

"I wish I could tell you that, but no. I didn't realize how bad things were until my mom got the call. You see, one night during winter break, my friend killed herself. She was sick of being bullied and didn't know how else to deal with it, is my best guess. She didn't leave a note, but there was a website up on her computer with a bunch of malicious lies about her and a naked picture that someone had taken in the locker room. What do you think happened to those girls?"

Gray stared at me for a long moment before finally speaking. "Hopefully they had to answer for their actions, right?"

"I wish I could tell you that, but no. Sure, they got in trouble for the website when it was traced back to them, but they didn't have to answer for her death. I have every faith that karma will get them in the end, but I didn't have to stick around that podunk town long enough to find out. After my parents kicked me out, Gams took me in. She made me go to college and gave me a family when my own didn't want my gay ass breathing their rarified air." At Gray's horrified look, I nodded sadly. "It's okay, Gray. I'm happy now."

He was wiping away tears again, breaking my heart with his sweetness. I patted his hand. "Don't cry for me, boo-boo. I hate to tell you that all parents aren't as supportive as your daddy, but you'd know I was lying if I tried to sell you that bill of goods. Don't worry about it, things worked out for me in the end. I have Gams and Beelzebub, don't I?

But that's a story for another day because we're getting off track here. My point in all this was to say that bullying doesn't just disappear. Things will always escalate, as you've already seen. I'm sure things probably started with name-calling before he ever threw the first punch. And now here you are, lying in a hospital bed. Where will it end, Gray? From where I'm sitting, it won't end well. And boo-boo? I can't attend another funeral for a teenager that I care about, you hear me?"

I sat there for a few minutes letting him digest what I'd said while I tried not to push him too hard. When he finally spoke, I had to strain to hear his whispered remark. "He calls me Gracie. And he said if I wanna be a little bitch, then he's gonna treat me like one."

My blood ran cold when I realized what he was saying. "What did he mean by that, Gray?" I squeezed his hand, offering what little comfort I could. "Has he tried to do anything more than hit you? Tell me, boo-boo. It won't leave this room, unless it needs to—and even then, I'll be by your side. But I need you to tell me, has that shithead tried to touch you in other ways?"

Gray avoided eye contact, staring out the window as he slowly nodded. "It all started when he caught me alone in the locker room one day and tried to kiss me. I said no and tried to walk around him, but then he grabbed my crotch and tried to feel me up. I kneed him in the balls, and that's what started our first fight. I don't know, maybe I had it coming? I mean, I did start it when I kneed him."

"No, fuck that shit. Look at me, boo-boo. I need you to hear what I'm saying." I waited until he hesitantly turned to look at me. "No means no. You were in the right to protect yourself after telling him no. And I'll be happy to explain it myself to that closeted mofo if I ever get the chance."

His eyes went wide. "Do you think that's the problem? He's in the closet?"

I pursed my lips as I nodded. "That's my guess, since he tried to kiss you. But who knows? At any rate, he's not our problem—you're the kid that we care about around here." As I leaned forward and carefully hugged him again, I realized that every word I'd said was true. I really did care about this kid.

After I sat up again, Gray reached for a tissue to blow his nose. We both shared a cleansing laugh when he honked into the tissue. After he tossed it into the bin, he settled back again and stared at me thoughtfully for a moment. "Is it weird that I don't know if I'm into boys or not? I might be, because there are a few that I think are cute. But I like girls too. Do you think maybe I'm bi like my dad? All I know is that I definitely didn't want my first kiss to be with Clark." He gasped after accidentally saying the name, but I simply held up a hand.

"I'm not going to repeat that, boo-boo. That's for you to tell, unless you don't, in which case I'll have to tell your dad. And as for whether or not you like boys? You have plenty of time to figure all that out. Just remember, nobody has the right to push themselves on you—no matter who they are."

16

CORBIN

After hearing the full story from Gray after Andy finally got him to talk, I was waiting in the school office bright and early Monday morning with Andy and Gray. We'd waited until after first bell so that Gray didn't have to see any of the kids. But I wanted that fucking principal to look at my bruised and battered son and tell me to my face that he was equally at fault. Their anti-bullying policies sucked and hadn't done shit to protect my son.

Principal Johnston was an older man, and while we hadn't had many run-ins, I'd always found him to be a by-the-book kind of guy. After greeting us with a polite handshake, he led us all into his office and took a seat behind his desk while we got settled in the visitors' chairs. "Good morning, Dr. Davis." He turned to Gray, lifting a brow, concern clear in his eyes. "I must admit that I'm surprised to see you here, Grayson; surely you're not staying for classes today? My secretary informed me that you were in the hospital over the weekend, after the unfortunate incident at the dance. While I apologize for what you endured, I am glad to see that you're up and around."

I held up a hand for Gray to remain quiet. "No, we're not here for Grayson to attend classes, and we can forego the pleasantries. We're here because I want you to take a good look at my son and see what happened to him while attending a function on school property." Gray stared at the floor, too embarrassed to look at his principal. The poor kid had really freaked out about coming here today, but I'd been firm. I wanted them to see what they'd allowed to happen to him with their bullshit policies.

"Dr. Davis, I understand that you're upset—"

Holding up a hand, I stopped him mid-sentence. "No, Mr. Johnston. You don't get it. I'm not upset—I'm livid. I want to make sure that your office isn't going to sweep this under the rug until that Neanderthal shit-prick of a Danvers kid ends up raping my kid. Shit, he gave him a concussion this time. The next time he might accidentally kill him. I haven't followed up with the police investigation yet, but they're next on my list. This needs to end before somebody gets even more hurt. If he gets off scot-free on this one, who knows what he'll try next."

He started to answer, but whatever he'd planned to say was interrupted when his secretary knocked and opened the door. She shot a smug look in my direction before looking at her boss. "My apologies, sir. Mr. Danvers is out here, and he is rather insistent that he be allowed to attend this meeting."

Well, I guess I don't need to wonder how Danvers found out that we're here. Mr. Johnston turned to me hesitantly, but I simply waved a hand. "I'll allow it. I'd like to hear what he has to say about what his son did to mine."

Gray looked up at me with panic written across his face. Shaking his head, he leaned forward to whisper. "I don't want to see him, Dad. Please don't let them bring Clark in here. I can't look at him right now."

Principal Johnston heard him and was quick to call out after the secretary. "Linda, only Mr. Danvers. There's no reason to disturb Clark from his studies, or disrupt our meeting any further."

She held the door open, motioning for Harold Danvers to join us. Even larger than his son, his muscle had gone to fat to the point that his gut came through the door first, propped up by a large silver belt buckle. I took a steadying breath, forcing myself to remain calm as he casually looked my son over as though it were just another Monday morning. Linda came bustling back in with another chair, setting it off to the side of the principal's desk so that he wasn't sitting with us—thank fuck. I doubt it was for our benefit, but I was grateful nonetheless.

After he'd wedged himself into the chair, Harold picked a piece of nonexistent lint off his polyester pants before sneering at my and Andy's joined hands. I hadn't even realized that I'd reached for Andy's hand until I saw Harold notice. His thick, gray mustache shoved up against his nostrils as his lip curled with disgust. "I should've known a queer kid was probably learning that shit at home."

I was halfway out of my chair when Mr. Johnston held up a hand. "Allow me, Dr. Davis. Now Mr. Danvers, we've allowed you to attend this meeting as a courtesy. Please keep any disparaging comments to yourself. This school firmly supports equal rights for all of our students. Perhaps we could begin with your purpose in joining us today?"

"Bah! Isn't it obvious? I had no choice but to get involved after a pair of cops came knocking on my door yesterday. We'd just got back from Sunday services, if you can believe the nerve of them. My son barely slept a wink last night. Now since my son's had a few scuffles with this freak, I want to make sure that he's not being blamed by this fine institution for the unfortunate incident Friday night." I rolled my eyes at Harold's turn of phrase. *Why the fuck does everyone keep calling this case of outright assault an unfortunate incident?* Harold turned to point a finger at me. "Keep in mind that I have more than one attorney on retainer before you make any libelous claims, Davis."

My mouth fell open as I gaped at the man's gall. "Excuse me? I beg your pardon, but it's not libel if it's the truth, Danvers. And the fact that you don't seem to be concerned by the fact that your son beat mine to the point of unconsciousness is more than a little disturbing. It wasn't an *unfortunate incident*." I punctuated that last thought with finger quotes, then paused to take a calming breath before continuing in a deceptively conversational tone. "It was assault—plain and simple. Say what you will, I have every faith the police in our town will get to the truth, sooner or later."

Danvers leaned forward with a smug smirk on his face. "Do you now? And I'm assuming that you have evidence to back up this claim that you're presenting as fact?"

I motioned toward Gray. "Yes, I have the victim's firsthand account."

Harold settled back in his chair, smiling triumphantly. "And that right there is where we have a problem, Davis. You see, my son denies having had anything to do with it. When I heard about your kid's injuries, it was only natural that I questioned Clark first, given the bad blood between our kids. But he's assured me that he wasn't anywhere near your son that night. Unless any other witnesses come forward, who's to say which kid is telling the truth? The school's records will back up the fact that our kids were found equally at fault in their previous incidents. Clark did his suspension after their last dust-up, and lost privileges to play football this semester. I'd say he's paid his dues, wouldn't you? I don't know what your kid thinks he's going to get out of blaming my son for his misfortunes. Without any proof, I'd be a pretty awful father if I didn't take my own son's word for it. But if you don't want to take my word for it, why don't you ask the fine, upstanding officers who came by our home yesterday to take Clark's statement? They didn't seem to find anything out of place with what he had to say on the subject. My son's a victim in this too, when you get right down to it. The poor kid. You know it had to have scared the shit out of him to find two cops at our door. He didn't even have an appetite last night."

Ignoring his bluster, I turned to Principal Johnston. "Is what he's saying true? Are you really going to allow this to be a case of Gray's word against Clark's, and not make the Danvers kid answer for what he did? If you do, that's just as criminal as what he did to my son." I turned to point a finger at Harold. "And as for your son missing football? Football ended three weeks ago, as you damn well know. He's not missing out on anything. As for that five-day suspension, he probably enjoyed the break."

Harold merely shrugged, while Principal Johnston held out his hands. "Dr. Davis, I'm sure you can see that my hands are tied. When you follow up with the police, they'll assure you that they need the same thing we do—proof that Clark committed the crime. Without any other witnesses coming forward and no physical evidence, there's really nothing the school can do. It would have been a different matter if someone had caught the aggressor in the act, but at this point, it truly is Clark's word against Grayson's."

My stomach churned when I heard Gray softly crying.

Andy turned to wrap his arms around him while I fought to keep my cool. "I don't care how big that kid is, he couldn't have punched Gray as much as he did without at least having bruised knuckles. But you know what? Never mind. I'll just mention that when I'm down at the police station. Maybe they'll be more interested in actually looking for physical evidence."

Danvers snorted. "You think them cops who came by our house didn't ask about that? Shoot, get over yourself, Davis. My kiddo trains every day. He's always got bruised or split knuckles. Damn boy can't be bothered to tape his hands up before he works the bag some days. And don't forget, unlike your son who sits home playing with makeup like a little girl, mine comes home to do chores and work around the family farm. You probably wouldn't know this, but real men get bruises. You go right ahead and run this false accusation to the police, I can't stop you. Just know that my lawyers will have a field day with you." He smirked as he lifted a hand to scratch his stubbled chin. "And I doubt there's even any physical evidence left in that bathroom by this point. The janitor here does a real fine job with bleach, or so I've been told. Not that there wouldn't be a million different reasons for my son's prints to have been found there, since this is just as much his school as it is your kid's. I think what needs to happen is for our kids to learn to coexist. Maybe your pansy-ass little girly-boy here needs to learn to not rile his classmates up so much, if he's finding himself in these situations."

I held up a hand. "That's quite enough, Danvers. You need

to shut your filthy mouth before I shut it for you." My temper was hanging by a very thin thread, but my stomach sank when I realized the truth of his words. They really weren't going to do anything about this situation, and it was highly doubtful that we'd solve it through legal means either. I leaned forward and put both hands on Mr. Johnston's desk. "We're done here, thank you for your time. You've left me with no recourse. I'm withdrawing my son from your school. Tell your secretary to pull his records, I'll be taking his file with me when we leave your office."

Gray gasped, pulling away from Andy to stare at me. "Dad! No! You can't do that to me. Becca is my only friend and she'll still be here. I can't leave her alone now that Clark knows I talked. Besides, where will I even go to school?"

I shook my head. "I'm sorry, kiddo. I know you're not going to like my answer, but I'm going to have to put you into the private school across town. You can be mad at me all you want, but your safety is paramount to me. If these assholes aren't going to look out for you, then I damn well will."

Principal Johnston was sputtering but I ignored him as I stood and motioned for Andy and Gray to head for the door. We were done here. After a quick word in my ear, Andy took Gray to wash his face and clean out his locker while I collected his file. Gray would be pissed at me for a while, but I gave less than a shit about that. The only thing that mattered was finding a way to keep him safe.

Thankfully, Danvers stayed behind in Mr. Johnston's office while Linda took care of the paperwork for me to withdraw him from their school. By the time I walked out of the office, Andy was quietly escorting an angry-looking Gray to the car.

Gray didn't look at me, much less say a word, the entire way home. I wasn't at all surprised to find Dana there when we arrived. She lifted a brow when Gray stormed past her and went straight for his room, slamming his door behind him. "I'm guessing your meeting went well? I hope you don't mind, but I took the liberty of letting myself in. I took today off so I could give you a hand with Gray."

I led the two of them into the kitchen and put on a pot of coffee while Dana puttered around looking for my teapot. Andy took a seat at the big island counter and sat there quietly, looking pensive as he chewed his lip. Once the coffee was done brewing, I poured us each a cup and joined Andy at the counter. "Let me guess, you don't approve of the move I made either?"

Dana looked curious, but didn't ask any questions while I waited for Andy's response. He finally heaved a sigh and looked at me with a sad smile. "I want to tell you that you screwed up, because Gray should have a say in where he goes to school at his age. But at the same time, I can't help but support your decision. There was absolutely no way you could have left him in a school where they'd allow him to be assaulted and not lift a finger to place blame even when Gray took the risk of coming forward to name his attacker. It's just a hell of a mess, boo." He reached out and rested his hand over mine, giving it a squeeze before continuing. "I get it, but damn, this sucks. That was an awful big step to take in the middle of your son's sophomore year, and I know it wasn't an easy decision for you to make. I hope you know that things are gonna be dicey between the two of you for a minute until he realizes that you did the right thing."

I looked up when I heard Dana let out a low whistle. "Holy hell, Corb. You really pulled him out of Rockford High? Go big or go home, huh?"

"Damn straight I did. Harold Danvers showed up and insisted on joining us, making it clear that his attorneys would wipe their ass with me if I made *libelous claims* toward his son. Principal Johnston went right along with him. They basically said that without another witness, it would come down to a case of he said, he said. And naturally, Danvers had reasonable excuses for why his son's knuckles would be bruised or split when the cops looked them over."

Dana's nostrils flared as she blew out a breath. "At least the cops questioned the punk, that's something at least. He'll be on their radar now, not that it helps much at the moment. Hmm. Maybe I'll see what I can do to pull Becca out too. It might be tight, but I'm sure I can figure something out. I'm guessing you're planning on putting him in the private school, yeah?"

"Yeah, that's the plan. It's not like we have any other

options." I caught her eye, smiling sadly. "You know, it is okay to separate our kids. I realize they've always been joined at the hip, but you don't need to make her suffer over a decision I made. I didn't have a choice, Dana. I have to put him first and the school has proven that they can't be trusted with his safety."

She nodded emphatically. "Oh, don't you dare apologize. I completely agree. But see, here's the thing. Becca doesn't have any other friends either. The two of them will probably need each other to make it through high school. But more importantly, she is going to be a walking target because of her proximity to Gray. You know that little shit-stain is going to be coming for blood, even if he did get off scot-free. I can't risk her safety either."

"Do I dare suggest asking her sperm donor to help? I know he's a shitty father, but surely you can get Larry to pony up for his share of her educational expenses." I winced at the familiar fury that passed through her eyes at the mention of her ex-husband.

Andy's eyes slowly moved back and forth between us as he set his coffee aside. "I feel like there's a story there, but that can wait for another day."

The spoon clinked against the cup while Dana stirred the honey into her tea with a little more force than necessary. She tossed her hair over her shoulder with an exaggerated eye roll. "Honey, please. I'd need a week to properly tell you that one. He's nothing like his brother. Although..." Her voice trailed off as she turned to look at me with a hint of excitement in her eyes. "Nick might be willing to give me a hand, now that I think about it. He always tells me that if I ever need anything for Becca to just give him a holler."

Andy perked up. "Wait, I forgot about that connection. That's how Gray was family to Nick. Because he's friends with Nick's niece! Okay, that makes sense now. I don't know why I never asked. I'm sorry, carry on." He grinned and wiggled his fingertips as if shooing the conversation back on track.

When Dana looked confused, I found myself laughing despite the stress of the past few days. "It's a long story, but here's the condensed version—when I ignored your advice and went looking for help at Saint's Place, Nick introduced me to Kandi and told her that Gray was family to him."

"Oh, okay. Yeah, that makes sense," Dana said with a light laugh. She turned to Andy with a fond smile. "Nick and my ex haven't spoken in years. In fact, I never even met Nick until after our divorce. He'd heard through the grapevine that his brother had left his family and simply showed up on my doorstep one night. Becca was all of eight years old at the time. She was a little girl who'd been starved for attention after living with a father who was never around, and he was all alone in the world, from what I could see. She and her uncle Nick were instant friends. He's taken her on camping trips and vacations to places like New York City at Christmas and Disney World on summer breaks. And once he heard about her best friend, Gray was included every time."

Andy nodded with an affectionate smile. "Yeah, that sounds like St. Nick. So how about you make Kandi real popular down at the bar and give me the four-one-one on him? I'd love to have some tea to spill on that sweet hunk of man candy. Nobody knows what his deal is, and he's sure not talking."

Dana shook her head. "Honey, if I knew, I'd be happy to share. But I don't know myself. His past is his own and I've never seen him date anybody. You probably know about as much as I do, to be honest." She stopped and gasped with delight as she walked over to the counter with her perfect cup of tea. "It just dawned on me! Oh, this is fabulous. Your drag name is Kandi?" She stopped on a giggle before going on. "Oh. Em. Gee. This is too cute for words. Does that mean that I can call you Kandi-Andy?"

"Definitely not." Andy was quick to shut that down. "The only person who dares call me that is my drag mother, and that's just because nobody can say no to her stanky ass." He stopped for a second and slapped his palm on the counter with a shout of laughter. "No, my gawd! I just realized that your ex, and Nick's asshole brother, is named Larry. Holy shit! That's hilarious because that's the real-life name of my drag mother. I bet Nick secretly loves that shit. No wonder he lets Honey get away with murder in there."

Dana nearly busted a gut laughing. When she came up for

air, tears were streaming down her face. "Oh, hell. If you only knew how homophobic my ex was, you'd be laughing even harder. That's priceless! A genderbending queen named Larry? Fuck, I love the irony. Holy shit. I can't wait to meet her someday because Corb told me about the swinging snake. Lord, I wish I'd been there to see that one. But what I want to know is why neither of you got a picture. Pics or it didn't happen, you know? But seriously. Let's get back to the Kandi-Andy of it all. If that name doesn't work for you, then how about Kandrew-Andrew? I could live with that." She shot Andy a playful wink while I laughed at the two of them.

Andy wagged his finger with a wide grin. "Sorry, honey. That won't work because my name is not Andrew."

"It's not?" I whipped around to look at him in surprise. "Why didn't I know that? It feels like I should've known something this basic, if you're supposed to be my boyfriend. Dare I ask what your name is, or is Andy actually what's printed on your birth certificate?

Andy shuddered. "Lawd, have mercy. I may be from the sticks, but even we're more refined than that, boo. Fine, I'll tell you, but prepare yourself." He sat up straight and lifted his nose in the air, laying on the Southern accent. "Allow me to properly introduce myself. Anderson Linwood Ferguson, at your service. And if either of your sorry asses ever dares call me that, you'd better be awful mad at me. Just don't expect me to answer to it."

I was smiling so hard that my cheeks nearly burned from

the stretch. "Anderson Linwood Ferguson? That's quite a moniker you got there, babe. Just tell me one thing, why would your parents name you something like that and then have the nerve to be shocked when you wound up being gay?"

Andy rolled his eyes. "I know, right? It truly is the perfect name for a gay man with my Southern charm. If I weren't so attached to certain people here in Rockford Bluff, I'd be tempted to move my happy ass to Atlanta and live it up."

Dana looked curious as she giggled. "Why Atlanta? That seems oddly specific."

"Isn't it obvious, *sugah*?" Andy drawled out his words, laying that honeyed accent on thick again. "Atlanta has a popping gay community, and where else in the country would they appreciate a historical name such as mine? Why, I'd be gay royalty, honey."

"You're honestly too adorable for words," Dana said to Andy before turning to me and batting her lashes with puppy dog eyes. "I see why you like him so much. Please tell me we're keeping him?"

With Dana there to keep an eye on Gray, I was free to give Andy a ride home. When I pulled into his driveway and put the engine in park, Andy reached over and turned off the car. I turned to look at him with a lifted brow. "I take it I'm not leaving just yet?"

Andy shook his head, unbuckling his seatbelt to lean a little closer. "No, I feel like this entire weekend has been a little too stressful for you, and rightfully so. I thought maybe we could take a few minutes and just breathe." He tilted his head back with a coy smile. "I wouldn't say no to a kiss, if you were so inclined."

I thought about that for half a second. Would I be an asshole if I sat here and made out a little bit with Andy after everything that had gone down today? Hell, since Friday. But on the other hand, I was allowed to have a moment for myself, wasn't I? I undid my own seatbelt and reached up to cup my palm around the side of his jaw as I smiled back at him. "As a cardiologist, I can attest that stress relief is good for the heart."

Andy widened his eyes, giving me his most innocent look as he leaned into my hand. "That's exactly what I was thinking! I'm offering myself purely for medicinal purposes, when you think about it."

"Well, I suppose that fits. I mean, according to Loretta, you can be a bit of a pill." I was still laughing as I closed my lips over his for a kiss. I wasn't sure how chaste I'd expected it to be, but I didn't anticipate his hands immediately sliding under my shirt to explore my chest while his tongue slipped into my mouth.

"Mhmm," I moaned into his mouth. I was also letting my own hands do the talking by this point, pushing his T-shirt up to let my fingers explore his slim physique. I was so lost in our kiss that when I heard the rasp of a zipper, it took me a moment to realize it was mine. I jerked back, breaking the kiss and staring down in shock as he pulled my rock-hard cock out—right there in front of God and anybody who might be watching.

I gaped as Andy merely gave me a slow, flirty wink before lunging forward and licking the tip. He had half of my shaft in his mouth by the time I found my voice. "Andy, what are you doing?" I whisper-yelled.

Pulling away from my cock with an audible pop, Andy turned to look up at me. The string of saliva connecting his lips to the head of my cock didn't fall away until he spoke. "If you have to ask, then I'm not doing it right, boo. Why don't you lean back in your seat and take your medicine like a man? Dr. Love is in the office and he's written you a prescription for desperately needed stress relief."

I looked around with wild eyes when he went back down and started to lick the prominent ridge along my shaft. "But your grandmother... what if she looks out the window? And... I mean... Andy! What about the neighbors?" I groaned as he took me back into the heat of his mouth, humming around my shaft as he swallowed my cock all the way down to the root.

He pulled back up and kissed the tip before returning his gaze to me for a moment. "Gam-Gam rarely gets out of her chair, let alone looks out the window. As for the neighbors, they're welcome to watch if they want. Now hush, honey. Tilt that seat back and let Dr. Love take care of you."

When he opened his jaw and sucked me back in, I fumbled for the seat release and did just as he'd requested. I couldn't argue with him—sometimes a person really did need to take their medicine like a man. I closed my eyes as I leaned back, one hand resting on the back of his head, gently pushing it up and down while my other hand crept down his spine and slipped under his waistband.

Andy moaned around my cock, arching his back when my fingertip grazed over his hole. I pulled my hand back out long enough to suck on my middle finger and give it a little moisture before slipping it back down where it belonged. When I tapped against his entrance, Andy pushed back, groaning as my finger slid into his heat.

He made a series of grunts that I deciphered as him asking what I was doing. Leisurely pumping my finger in rhythm with his head, I stared at the starbursts behind my closed eyelids and smiled. "You're not the only one who can prescribe stress relief, babe. Now suck my cock while you take your medicine like a man, Dr. Love."

I shivered with delight when Andy started laughing, the vibrations tingling all along my length. As I gave in to the moment, the world fell away until it was just the two of us. I figured Andy had a point. If anybody wanted to watch, they could have at it—but I wasn't giving up this moment for anything.

It seemed like it was only a matter of seconds before I was coming into Andy's eager mouth, but who could say? Time didn't exist in our private little bubble. The only things I was aware of were that bewitching tongue and the heat of a certain hole that I was already eager to spend more time exploring.

My body felt numb as I jerked forward into a curl, crying out Andy's name as liquid heat exploded in my core. As feeling slowly returned to my limbs, spreading out into my shaky arms and twitchy legs, I tugged Andy up into my arms for a kiss.

I moaned as he parted his lips and his cum-soaked tongue slid against mine. Tasting myself in his mouth was a whole new level of hotness that I couldn't remember ever having experienced. But then again, was anything ever the norm with this cutie?

17

ANDY

"Hey, stranger. I sure did miss you this weekend." I shot Corbin a playful pout. He'd just shown up for his morning coffee and, as usual, was looking finer than a frog's hair. "How's our kiddo? I'm guessing you two didn't kill each other on your little fishing trip this weekend, since you seem to be in one piece and I don't see any blood splatter."

Corbin blew out a breath, raking his fingers through his hair as he rolled his eyes. "It was hit and miss at first, but the nice thing about being stuck on a boat in the middle of a lake is that eventually, you have to talk. I'm glad I decided to do it, even if he fought me on it. I think things are going to be a little smoother now. And he'll be in a good mood when I get home today, I imagine."

"That's right! I'd almost forgotten. Today was Becca's first day at the new school, right?" Since there were no other customers waiting and Tracy had already started his drink, I leaned against the counter and settled in for a bit of a chat.

"Yep. The two of them were texting like mad last night to coordinate their looks." Corbin shook his head, looking adorable in his confusion. "Can somebody please explain that to me, please? They have to wear uniforms now. What's there to coordinate? Isn't not having to worry about what you're wearing the whole point of having a uniform?"

Tracy and I shared an amused look before I turned back to Corbin with a sympathetic smile. "Aren't you precious, honey? I feel so bad for you sometimes. There's a whole lot more to your look than the clothes you're wearing. Are they wearing makeup? Wait, is makeup even allowed at the school? But yeah, they also have to worry about hair and hair accessories. And even the most mundane uniform can be jazzed up, I'll have you know. It's all in the presentation."

Corbin looked completely lost. "Yes to the makeup, I made sure of that before we registered him. But back to the jazzing thing. Tell me how the hell somebody jazzes up a uniform?"

Reaching over the counter, I patted his hand. "Don't worry your pretty little head about it, boo. Just take notice of how Gray looks when he comes and goes. You'll figure it out. So tell me, is he still going to try to get into the glee club?"

"Are you kidding me? He informed me that he wouldn't be home until after four-thirty because he and Becca were staying after for tryouts, and then he's going to wait with her while Becca signs up for the community awareness class he's been taking. It's a great program that gives them extra credit for volunteer work, while teaching the kids the joy of giving back. " He smiled his thanks to Tracy as she slid his drink across the counter before discreetly slipping away to busy herself with something behind us.

I waited while he took his first drink, smiling to myself at the way the tip of his tongue darted out to wipe away a stray blob of foam. I still couldn't believe that I'd been such a brazen little hussy as to go down on him in broad daylight a couple weeks ago, but I definitely didn't regret it. Just thinking about the way he'd fingered me made my butt tingle. I must have moaned or something because Corbin's eyes heated as he gazed back at me, accompanied by that cute little blush he got.

Rather than comment, he merely lifted a brow and winked at me as he took another sip of his coffee. I cleared my throat and discreetly adjusted myself before I attempted to say another word. "So, I've been thinking. It's been over two weeks now, maybe it's time we try that whole date thing again."

Corbin stared at me blankly for about half a second before his eyes widened with understanding. His blush deepened as a coy smile slowly spread over his face. "Well now, Mr.

Ferguson. Am I to believe that you are trying to ask me out for a date?"

I decided that I could be coy too. "Well now, I don't rightly know, Dr. Davis. Should I be asking you on a date? I mean, I wouldn't want to distract you from your busy schedule."

His eyes danced merrily as he chuckled. "Distract me all you want, babe. I'd like nothing better. Since you're the one doing the asking, does this mean that you will be doing the planning this time?"

My brows shot to my hairline. "I don't recall asking you anything yet, my dear sir. I merely questioned as to whether I ought to be asking, I didn't actually say—"

Tracy's hand shot out from the side to cover my mouth. "You two are being ridiculous. Obviously, you need a referee to step in or you'll never leave the batting cage. Wait, I'm not really that good with sportsball references. Would it make more sense to say that you'll never get enough yardage to make a pass? Or that you won't get to first base? Home court? Help me out here, guys. Actually, never mind. You get my drift. Corbin, let's just consider it a done deal that Andy has asked you out and you're saying yes. What day is good for you?"

She giggled and jerked her hand away when I licked her palm. "Girlfriend, are you really going to talk to two men about planning a date and then go and mention naughty phrases like making a pass, hitting first base, or... hell... you had me at batting." Corbin was laughing so hard he was gasping for air as I advanced on Tracy. "Are you sure you don't want to say anything about bats, sticks, or balls? What about tight ends, punting, making a squeeze play, or maybe even the deliciously dirty-sounding backdoor slider? I mean, we could go for days with sports innuendos."

Tracy held her hands up and backed slowly away from me. "I call uncle. I can't ever win an innuendo war with you, I was a fool for trying. Just remember not to pull the goalie and leave yourself unprotected." She defiantly jutted her chin out with a proud gleam in her eye as she remembered the hockey term right at the end there. Then she dropped her chin with another round of giggles. "Get it? The goalie is like a condom? He keeps the little pucks from making it into the net."

I sighed heavily, sadly shaking my head as if brokenhearted on her behalf. "You were so close, honey. You'd made a good one, and then you had to go and ruin it by explaining it. Girl. I don't even know where to begin with you."

Corbin cleared his throat, wiping a tear from his eye as he tried to get my attention. "You've got customers coming up, and I need to get upstairs anyway. As much as I hate to interrupt the Andy and Tracy show, we should probably wrap this up."

"That's exactly the point I was trying to make," Tracy said

with a beatific smile. "When you go on your date, make sure you remember to plan to wrap things up."

Corbin was blushing so hard; a person might think he had rosacea at this point. I decided to put him out of his misery. "Hey, boo. You think we can make plans this weekend for maybe lunch and a matinee? Or would dinner and a nighttime movie be better? Either way, we'd get to have food and then snuggle in a dark theater. How does that sound?"

"That sounds absolutely perfect," Corbin said as he picked up his drink and stepped to the side so the lady who'd walked up behind him could reach the register. I let Tracy deal with the customer while I moved over so we could finalize our plans. "Actually, remember that volunteering thing that I mentioned Gray is doing now? He has his first shift this Saturday from noon to four. Lunch and a matinee would be perfect, and then I can pick him up on my way home."

I somehow resisted the urge to squeal with glee now that we'd scheduled our date. Instead, I restrained myself to what I hoped passed for a nonchalant smile. "That sounds great then. We'll figure out the details later, I know you need to get going."

I was pretty sure that Corbin surprised both of us when he blew me a kiss as he backed away, because he almost immediately started blushing again. I bit the inside of my cheek to keep from laughing when he almost stumbled over his feet as he turned to go. Lifting his hand in a wave,

Corbin promised to text me later and made his way to the elevator.

As I watched the doors close behind him, I jumped when a damp towel snapped me on the ass. I gasped indignantly as I turned and grabbed the towel from Tracy's hand. A quick glance told me that the customer had left and the coast was clear before I snapped her back. "No, you didn't. Girl, why do you keep trying to start things with me today that you know you can't finish?"

Tracy giggled and made kissing noises before she started chanting. "Corbin and Andy sitting in a tree, K–I–S–S–I–N–G."

I bit back a laugh as I went to snap her again. "Just wait, little girl. Michael will be in later, remember? How many times do I have to tell you, honey? Payback's a bitch and so am I."

She laughed even harder as she flinched away from the towel. "You better be nice to me. I just helped you get your date set up. Just think, at this time on Saturday, you'll be getting all gussied up for your boo."

The towel fell to my side as I dropped my arm. "Well, shut my mouth. I can't argue with that one. Dammit, now I don't know what to say."

Tracy flashed me a wink as she turned to greet the customer walking up. "You could always start with thank you."

Clutching my hands to my chest, I batted my eyelashes and gave her my most angelic smile. "Thank you, Miss Tracy. You're a goddess among women."

Glancing back at me over her shoulder, Tracy shot me a shit-eating grin. "Tell me something I don't know, sweetie."

So far, this date had gone much smoother than our last. After a good lunch, we were snuggled up in the back row of the movie theater. We'd raised the armrest separating us so that I could lean against Corbin while we shared our popcorn. With his arm around my shoulder, I felt giddier than a schoolboy on his first date. When my buttery fingers grazed the bottom of the popcorn tub that sat in his lap, I began to make a dirty joke about needing a hole when my phone started to ring.

"Quick, shut it off before people around us get irritated, babe," Corbin needlessly whispered as I fumbled for my phone and muted the volume. Before I could respond, his phone went off in his pocket. I jerked back, feeling the vibration where our hips were touching. Corbin winced apologetically as he pulled his phone out. He took one look at the screen and grew serious. "It's the hospital, babe. I'm gonna have to step out in the lobby and take this." I nodded and rose to follow him, figuring I'd deal with my own call at the same time.

While he took a few steps away to answer his phone, I dug

mine out and found that Helen, Gams' caregiver, had been the one calling. Oh, shit. My heart raced as I called her back, drumming my fingers against my thigh and trying not to freak out while I waited for her to answer.

"Hello? Andy, is that you?" Her nasally voice killed me every time.

I rolled my eyes, resisting the urge to remind her that my contact information would've come up when I called. "Yeah, it's me. Is everything okay?"

"No, that's why I'm calling. I'm at the emergency room with your grandmother. She had another episode and fell down." She continued quickly, before I could interrupt. "They're looking for her doctor now, but an orthopedic specialist has already been in. They think she may have broken her hip when she fell."

Fuck. I blindly reached out to brace my hand against the lobby pillar. My entire body felt numb and my legs were trembling. I looked around the lobby, desperate to lay eyes on Corbin. When I saw him headed my way, I sucked in a relieved breath. "I'm actually with her doctor right now, let her know we'll be right there."

As Corbin walked up, his brows were drawn close over his obviously concerned gray eyes. "That was my service, we need to—"

I held up my phone and cut him off midsentence. "The hospital. I know. That was Helen who called me just now. Please, Corbin. Take me to Gams."

Without another word, he reached for my hand and laced our fingers together as we rushed out of the theater. I calmed down a little bit once I was in the car with Corbin, but when we got to the hospital, I was a mess all over again when he had to leave me at the front desk while he took off to do doctor things. While I waited impatiently for the nurse to get off the phone to answer my questions, Helen walked up and took my arm.

"There you are, Andy. Come with me, so I can let you know what's happening." Helen might've been about as useful as a steering wheel on a mule when we were at home, but she was obviously at her best in an emergency. The short, scrawny woman planted a hand on my lower back, guiding me to the waiting area with an iron grip. "Now I want you to sit down and let me fill you in on what's happening, okay? This will go much faster if I'm doing the talking and you're just listening."

I was too stunned by this new take-charge Helen to be offended by her brusque tone. "Yes, ma'am. Please, just tell me if Gams is all right."

Her nostrils flared as she took in a deep breath over pinched lips, as if to fortify herself. "Her heart is stable, but it was an arrhythmia that caused her to be lightheaded. They'll know more about that now that her cardiologist has arrived. But you need to prepare yourself. Your grandmother's going to need surgery to stabilize her hip. Her bones are so brittle that it's going to be hard on her. The recovery will be a nightmare, but I have every faith that she'll sail through. Loretta is much too stubborn to let a little thing like pain hold her back."

My fingers were itching to pull out my phone so I could start Googling information about hip replacements, but I forced myself to remain calm and kept my hands in my lap while Helen told me about the whole ordeal from the moment Gams had fallen until I'd arrived. When she stood and grabbed her purse, preparing to leave, I stared at her in shock. "Wait, you're not staying?"

Helen smiled kindly, but shook her head with a firm negative. "My job was to be a home health care provider for your grandmother. I've done that. When she returns home and is ready to resume her daily routine, contact the agency and they'll either send me or a replacement. I've already contacted my service and ended our contract. I have bills to pay, so unfortunately I'll need to move on to another patient."

I was confused. "Wait, I don't understand. Are you saying that Gams might be here in the hospital for a while?"

The smile she gave me was almost pitying. "Your grandmother has a long road ahead of her. The recovery she faces is going to be intensive. By my estimation, she won't be able to come home for at least a week, if that. And that's if they don't send her to a convalescent hospital. Your grandmother has major medical issues, and she is not a young woman. It's going to take at least a month, if not much longer, for her to get through this—but I need you to understand that it can take six months to a year for a patient like her to fully recover."

It felt so cold, the way she was just moving on. I'd never been a big Helen fan, but come on. A little bit of human kindness would be nice, even if she was off the clock now. Pushing back the ugliness that threatened to spill out of my mouth, I gave her my best Southern smile. "Thank you, Helen. You've been a real help to us, *bless your heart.*"

Once she was gone, I pulled out my phone and began researching. I didn't get truly scared until I saw an article that said that the mortality rates in the elderly were higher after breaking a hip. One in five geriatric patients died within a year of surgery? Fuck. I decided that Google could kiss my ass and put my phone away. Nope. I didn't need that kind of negativity in my life. Crossing my arms over my chest, I scooted down in the plastic, bucket-seated chair and leaned my head back against the wall. After I'd finished counting the ceiling tiles for the gazillionth time, I closed my eyes and sent up a prayer to whoever might be listening that my gam-gam would make it through this bullshit.

"Andy?" My eyes fluttered open at the sound of Corbin's voice, and I turned to see him sitting in the chair beside me. He looked weary, a fact not helped by the puke-green surgical scrubs he was wearing. I guessed I'd finally found a color that didn't work for my boo. He reached for my hand, smiling compassionately as he stroked his thumb over my knuckles. "How are you holding up, babe? Your grandmother's been moved into a private room. She's resting now, but I can take you to see her as soon as you're ready."

I sat up quickly, blinking rapidly as I came fully awake. "I don't know how I managed to fall asleep sitting here. Tell me, how is she?"

"She's doing about as well as can be expected. I was there monitoring her heart throughout the entire surgery. I told Dr. Evans that I'd fill you in on everything. I have his information for you, but it will also be in her paperwork. He's the orthopedic surgeon who stabilized her hip. I'm not going to lie to you, Andy. Her arrhythmia concerns me. We're going to keep her here for a while as we monitor her recovery. After a few days, we'll put together a plan and decide what her next steps will be. But all that can wait. Right now, why don't you just let me take you to her."

He stood, offering a hand to help me to my feet. I felt bereft when he dropped my hand, but I understood that this was his workplace. I felt slightly better when he rested a hand between my shoulder blades as he guided me through the halls. It dawned on me then that he was supposed to pick Gray up a long time ago. Thinking of that, I glanced up at him. "Where's Gray? I'm sorry we held you up."

"He's fine, he understands that this is just part of my job. Becca ended up being scheduled for the same volunteer shift, so Dana picked them both up and took them home with her." His professional smile, combined with the reminder that this was, in fact, his job, made me feel lonelier than ever. It occurred to me all at once that Corbin wasn't here for me, or because he was family to my gams, he was here as her physician. Just like Helen, he had a job to do. When he started to follow me into Gams' room, I stopped him with a hand to his forearm.

"I don't want to keep you, I know you have other things you need to do. I'll be all right, I'm just going to sit with Gams for the night." Corbin looked confused and started to shake his head, but I flashed him a gentle smile and girded my heart. "It's okay, Corbin. I've been down this road before, I know how to take it from here."

He looked uncertain, but didn't argue as he returned my smile. "If you're sure. Listen, is there anything I can do for you? Bring you dinner, check on Jeebus? Name it, I'm not just going to walk away and leave you here."

Oh, how I wished that were true. "Actually, if you wouldn't mind picking up the devil dog, that would be a load off my mind. There's a hidden key under the fake rock in the flower bed beside the front door. It's sitting behind a lawn gnome dressed in a hula skirt."

My heart skipped a beat at his familiar grin. "Because why wouldn't a gnome be wearing a hula skirt? All right, consider it done." He started to step away then turned back as I stood there watching him leave. "If you change your mind and want some company, I'm only a text or phone call away."

I nodded and lifted my hand with a half-hearted wave. I didn't want him to go, but this wasn't what our original agreement had entailed. And even with everything that had happened since then, we still weren't in any sort of place where he needed to hold my hand at my grandmother's bedside. Hell, maybe the universe was trying to tell us something when shit went down in our families every time we tried to go on an actual date. Once he was gone, I took a deep breath and pushed my way into Gam-Gam's room.

A strangled cry caught in my throat when I saw her lying there, looking so frail and tiny on her bed. Pulling a chair up beside her, I reached for her hand. Her tiny, withered hand was so cold, it frightened me a little. Wrapping it between mine, I rubbed it to warm it up a little while I watched her sleep.

Nurses came and went as the evening progressed. The night nurse brought me a pillow and blanket a little before midnight. After showing me how to open my chair into a sleeping position, she ducked out of the room, only to return a few minutes later with a few half-sized, off-brand cans of coke and some snacks. "It's not much, but I noticed you haven't left the room. This will at least tide you over until you feel comfortable enough leaving your grandmother so you can visit the cafeteria."

I smiled at the older woman's considerate act, and set everything on the tray table. "Thank you, I appreciate it. Let me know if I get in your way, okay?"

"Don't worry about it, sweetheart. We've all been here, or we will be at some point. Miss Loretta here is your family; I understand that you don't want her to be alone. You let me know if you need anything, and I do mean anything, you hear?" Her smile was so maternal, it made my heart pang for what might've been if my own mother hadn't been so blinded by her religion. After one last check on Gams, the nurse turned off the main light, just leaving a night light on in the room as she moved out into the hall, pulling the door almost closed behind her so that just a crack of light came in. After she left, I ate a few snacks, got my chair set up, and settled in.

I woke up at some point during the night when I heard Gams coughing. I was up in a flash, pouring her a cup of water and slipping in a bendy straw. "Here, Gams. Let's sit you up so you can have a little sip." Her eyes fluttered open as a weak smile curved her lips. She batted weakly for the buttons on the bed. "Stop that, now. Let me get that for you." She seemed to relax a little, waiting with a pained look in her eye while I got the remote for the bed and helped her sit up a little. When her eyes went wide, I knew we'd gone too far and lowered her just a touch. "That better, gorgeous? Come on, let's get your whistle wet." I helped her get the straw into her mouth, then held the cup in place while she took a few sips.

After she pulled away, she spoke in a raspy voice. "Here we are again, huh? I hope I didn't ruin your outing with Dr. Pain in the Ass."

"Don't you fret, you're way more important than any old date. How are you feeling?" After I set the cup down, I looked through the bin of goodies they'd left on her nightstand until I found the Chapstick. "Pucker up for me, beautiful. Those lips are looking dry."

She rolled her eyes but obediently pursed her lips to let me moisten them. While I set about brushing her hair and straightening her nightgown, she watched me with an affectionate gaze. "You're so good to me, Andy. How did I ever get so lucky? I know I talk a lot of trash, but I hope you know that I love you with all my heart."

I bent to gently hug her, kissing her cheek before I sat back down and reached for her hand. "I love you too, Gam-Gam. You're my best girl, aren't you? It's you and me and the devil dog against the world. If I can just get you to quit scaring me like this, then we'll be just fine."

At the mention of Beelzebub, her eyes filled with concern. "Where is my baby? Did you feed him before you came down here?"

I shook my head. "Corbin went and picked him up. He took your so-called sweet baby Jeebus home with him for the night. I figure between him and Gray, that little dog will be so spoiled, he'll never wanna come home again."

"That's a good man you've got there, princess. Don't you let him get away. They don't make men like him anymore, not that they ever really did. We old fogies just like to pretend that everything was fine and dandy back in our day. But trust me, honey—men have been assholes since the dawn of time, present company excepted." She patted my hand. "Princesses don't count, last I checked."

The happiness in her eyes made me feel uglier than a two-day-old dog turd for lying. Swallowing around the lump in my throat, I decided it was time to fess up. "Gams, he's not really my man. I was just pretending that he was my boyfriend so you'd quit worrying about me and talking about setting me up."

Gams snorted. "I don't care what you say, baby boy. I've seen how the two of you look at each other. You might've thought you were starting out trying to fool with an old woman, but Cupid pulled a trick on you. If the two of you aren't sweet on each other, I'll eat my hat."

I quirked a brow as I shot her a skeptical look. "Are you talking about that miniature hat-shaped chocolate confectionery that you got from those Red Hat ladies? I'm pretty sure those don't count. No, if you want to eat a hat, you need to get one of those bug-infested straw hats from a farmer, or a sweaty old trucker's hat."

Gams narrowed her eyes, too familiar with my evasive maneuvers by now. "Don't you start that bull puckey with me, princess. I know when you're trying to get me sidetracked. Now tell me, what's really keeping you from taking things to the next step with your doctor beau?"

I bit my lip, trying to decide how much I wanted to divulge. I finally just shrugged and blew out a breath.

"Every time we try and have a real date, something happens to cockblock us. If that's not a sign from the universe, then I don't know what you'd call it. The first time we tried to have a real date was the night that his son got beat to hell and back. Then we tried to have another date today, and you ended up in the hospital. Someone upstairs is trying to tell us something, I dare you to tell me otherwise."

After rolling her eyes with a derisive snort, Gams leaned back against her pillow and studied me for a moment. "Listen, brat. You can't hate religion on one hand, and then say that someone upstairs is ruining your life on the other. One of these days you're going to have to make up your mind; either you're on the God train, or you're not. But as for your man? Your messy dates aren't a sign of anything other than you taking too long between dates. Hell, check your damn horoscope before you go out if you have to, but don't give up on love, honey. You can give up on a lot of things in life, but don't ever give up on that."

I blinked back tears as I smiled. "I love you so much, Gams."

She patted my hand then motioned toward the bed remote. "I love you too, princess. How about you lower me a little bit so I can go back to sleep?"

After I got her settled, she slipped right into slumber while I lay in my little chair-bed and thought about our conversation. I must've dozed off at some point, because I woke up to a brightly lit room and Gams arguing with the morning nurse, telling her in no uncertain terms that she was going on record that she wouldn't be going into any damned care facilities for recovery. I yawned, keeping my mouth shut while my gams had her little snit-fit. I was pretty sure that a care facility was in her future, but I wasn't going to be the one to have that argument. All I knew was that I was happier than hell to see her still alive and kicking in the full light of day.

18

CORBIN

"What's going on with you, Corb? You've been acting like a zombie all week. What's wrong, did you and Andy have your first spat?" Dana and I were sharing lunch at the small deli across the street from our offices. I took a bite of the egg salad sandwich I hadn't wanted and set it back down, ignoring the taste of cardboard in my mouth as I chewed.

When she pushed her own sandwich aside to reach for my hand, worry lines etched across her forehead, I blew out a breath and allowed her to hold my hand for a moment. "No, it's not that. At least, I don't think so? We didn't have a fight, but nothing's been the same since his grandmother got sick. It's like he's so worried about her that he's shut himself off from everyone and everything."

"Is he working? I didn't notice when I passed the coffee cart this morning. Surely he isn't having to stay by her bedside, right?" Dana didn't understand the depth of devotion that Andy felt for his grandmother. It had never been a matter of him having to be at Loretta's side, it was more a matter of him needing to be near her.

"No, he's definitely working. But get this shit. You know how I always stop by to see him for my morning coffee and flirt session? Every day this week when I've gone to the cart, he's let Tracy wait on me while he takes out trash or mops the floor or some shit. Today he got busy on a phone call with a supplier or something when I walked up. I feel like he's avoiding me, and I don't understand what's going on."

Dana pulled her sandwich closer again and studied it for a moment as she gathered her thoughts. She bit her lip as she looked up at me with pity in her eyes. "What about the dog, aren't you still taking care of him? That would be a way to get him to talk to you."

I shook my head. "No, the day after Loretta was admitted, I went to see him at the hospital, but he'd gotten a ride home. I was worried, because I remembered that we'd been on a date when everything went down so he didn't have his own car there, you know? But he's so fucking self-sufficient. He just handled everything without even so much as a text. While I was at the hospital looking for him, he stopped by the house and picked up Jeebus."

"That is weird," Dana said after swallowing her bite. "Did he say anything to Gray?"

I held up my hands. "How the hell should I know? I tried

to ask Gray about it, but he looked at me like I was weird and said that everything was normal. It's not like I was going to give him the third degree like some schoolgirl wanting to know if her crush likes her back."

Dana's eyes twinkled with suppressed laughter. "You never know, that might have gotten a little further with him. There's nothing kids love more than drama. Becca adores gossiping with me. I bet she'd be all over this, if she knew you needed help."

"That's just it." I wrinkled my nose at the sandwich, wondering if I should force it down when I didn't seem to have an appetite. How could I when the sun had gone out of my sky? Everything had been gray and sad without Andy around. "There hasn't been any drama. I don't understand what's wrong. Things were looking up and I thought we were starting to get somewhere, you know? But then Loretta got sick and Andy shut me out. I'd understand if her life was in danger, but she's doing well. Yes, she got hurt and needs to be closely monitored, but I believe she'll be fine once she's recovered."

"Is Kandi doing the show tonight? It is Thursday, you know. Maybe if you showed up down there you'd have better luck. It's worth a shot," Dana said with a shrug.

I thought about that for a moment then shook my head. "I don't want to look like a stalker. He hasn't been returning my texts or calls, he's avoiding me when I go to his cart— doesn't that tell you that he's avoiding me? Hell, if we didn't work in the same place and I wasn't his grandmother's doctor, the guy would probably have ghosted me completely. I don't know what I did, but whatever it was, I'm pretty sure it ended our fledgling relationship before it really began."

Dana arched her brow with a skeptical look on her face. "Fledgling, my ass. That man was there for you during Gray's time of need. Your relationship may not have been what you wanted it to be, but you two were definitely friends. Shit, why are we talking in the past tense already? Maybe he just needs a little space. I don't think you should write things off just because things have been weird for a few days."

"Five days, Dana. Five fucking days of silence. That's not things being weird, that's Andy telling me to piss off. I don't know how else I should take it, do you?" Closing the paper over my sandwich, I shoved the tray away. I was definitely done.

"Well for starters, I don't think you should take it lying down. If you want to try and have something with him, you need to fight for it. Make him talk to you and get some answers. Maybe he doesn't know that you even care one way or another. Hell, who knows what goes on in another person's mind." She paused to take a sip of her iced tea, holding up a finger to let me know she wasn't done yet.

After draining her cup and blotting her mouth, she looked off to the side for a moment as if trying to remember what she'd meant to say. "You know what? I can't help but wonder if maybe he doesn't just feel guilty because you guys were on a date when his grandmother got hurt."

"What? No... do you think? That doesn't make any sense, what would that have to do with anything?"

Dana rolled her eyes. "Sweetie, just because it doesn't make sense to you doesn't mean that's not how he's feeling. I'm not saying it is, but it's a reasonable concern." Her eyes widened as another thought occurred to her. "I bet I'm right. Think about it, Corb. What happened on your first date? Gray got hurt. And then you had a second date, and what happened? His grandmother got hurt. Shit, maybe he's superstitious and afraid to jinx it if you try for a third."

I stared at her for a moment as I turned that around in my mind. I hated to admit that it kinda made sense. "You think it's that easy? Because that actually makes *me* feel a lot better. Not because he might feel that way, don't get me wrong. But if whatever is going on was caused by things outside of my control, rather than something I said or did, then that's a load off my mind." I drummed my fingers on the table for a moment as I thought about that some more. "Shit, if that's the problem, what the hell do I do to fix it?"

Dana took a deep breath. "Now that is a tough one, and I don't have an easy answer for you. But in my opinion? I'd keep pushing him. Normally that's the opposite of the advice I give, but if you don't want him to push you away or shut you out completely, putting yourself in his face might be your best bet. Either way, at least you'll know you tried."

19

ANDY

"You know what? Maybe you should suck on a lemon so you have a reason for that scowl," Tracy commented as she watched me angrily sweeping the floor. "And while I'm already risking your wrath, can I just point out that when you slap the broom around like that, you're just making a bigger mess than you started out with in the first place? Talk to me, sweet thing. Tell Miss Tracy what's got your panties in a bunch."

I threw the broom to the floor, wincing at the clatter it made against the tile. "Sweeping is stupid. Work is stupid, customers are stupid, and..." I sighed as I bent to pick up the broom and resume sweeping, this time doing it properly. "Mostly? I'm stupid."

Tracy bit the side of her bottom lip as she watched me with a concerned frown. "This is about Dr. Hottie, isn't it? Honeybun, are you going to tell me what happened there?

You've been avoiding that poor man all week and the look he gets on his face every time you ignore him just breaks my heart. He's like a sad little boy who's been denied dessert while everyone around him eats cake."

Setting the broom aside, I scrubbed a hand over my face as I leaned against one of our small storage cabinets. "What happened is that I never should've gotten turned around by a pretty face and forgotten the one person who's never let me down. As for Corbin, he'll get over it. It's not like he was serious about me. Sure, we kissed a couple times and he let me blow him, but the only reason things between us ever even made it that far was because I pushed. He wasn't showing any signs of wanting anything deeper, was he? Damn Tracy, what the hell was I thinking?"

Tracy's mouth fell open, her eyes blinking rapidly as she took in what I'd said. "Okay, first of all? Too much information, but thank you for sharing because that's fucking hot as hell to imagine. But I don't understand. How did you forget the one person who never let you down? I'm assuming you're referring to your grandmother, right? Honey, just because you were on a date when she got hurt doesn't put that on you. The same thing could have happened if you'd been home. It was just shitty timing that you happened to be out doing something for yourself for once."

Wrapping my arms around my waist, I tucked my chin against my chest as I hugged myself, trying not to cry. "You don't understand, Tracy. People don't stay in my life. Except for Gams. She's the one person who's been there no matter what. I always take things further than they're supposed to go, and obviously I've done it again. People don't stay in my life, they move on when they get bored. Hell, my own family didn't want me around once they found out who I really am. Yeah, Corbin might be different, but I don't know if I have it in me to take the risk."

Tracy sniffed and threw herself at me, knocking my arms away and replacing them with her own as she wrapped me in a bear hug. "Count me with your gams, because I'm not going anywhere either. We're not just coworkers, you're my bestie. And yeah, maybe you've dated some losers or people who were too stupid to appreciate what they had. But honey, how do you know that Corbin might not be different if you don't give him a chance? You can't measure him with the same yardstick as the people you dated in the past. That's not fair to anyone. I'm pretty sure you wouldn't want him to compare you to his deceased spouse, would you?"

As she pulled back, I reached up to boop her nose. "Well, it might be interesting if he tried, considering that his spouse was a woman."

Tracy narrowed her eyes, playfully glaring at me as she poked me in the side. "You know that's not what I meant, you big booger. Seriously, Andy. Don't be that guy. Don't hold him responsible for things that people have done to you in the past. Just because other people have left, doesn't mean that he will. At the very least, don't you think you owe it to him to tell him how you feel?"

I shook my head as I squeezed past her. "I can't risk it, honey. It will hurt way too much when it's over if I go and let myself fall tragically in love with Dr. Hottie and his adorable son. Hell, I'm already half in love with the kid. He's too sweet for words, you know? Nope. I can't risk it."

The dust hadn't settled on our conversation when Corbin showed up at the cart for his morning coffee. I looked over my shoulder to get Tracy to step in like she had every other day this week, but the little hussy had disappeared. Painting a fake smile on my face, I took a deep breath and decided to suck it up.

Corbin froze like a deer in the headlights when he realized that I'd be serving him today. "Andy? Thank fuck. I've been worried sick about you, babe. Are you okay? Do you have a minute so we can we talk?"

I shook my head and stepped over to the espresso machine, flipping the switch to get it ready while I poured the milk into his cup. "I'm just fine, thanks for asking. You don't need to worry about little ol' me. By the way, in case Gray forgot to pass it on? Thank you so much for looking after Beelzebub for me. I appreciate that, more than you know." I spoke lightly, trying to keep things on a surface level.

When I went back to the counter with his drink, Corbin caught my hand before I could pull it away. "Can we cut the bullshit, please? I'm pretty sure we moved past that a long time ago, don't you think? What's going on with you, babe? Will you at least tell me why you've been ghosting me?"

I yanked my hand away as I lashed out at him. "Don't do that. Don't call me babe like I mean something to you, Corbin. We were just fake, remember? Gams is sick now, and it's all my fault. If I'd been home, she wouldn't have fallen. That piece of shit Helen didn't keep as close an eye on her as I would have if I hadn't been off gallivanting with you."

Corbin held up a hand. "You need to stop that line of thought in its tracks. You can't know that things would've been any different if you'd been there. You're allowed to have a life, Andy. There's nothing wrong with having been on a date when bad things happened. I didn't blame you or our date because I wasn't there when Gray got hurt. Bad things happen to good people. That doesn't have anything to do with our relationship, babe."

"Lord have mercy, will you quit calling me that?" I shook my head, sick at heart to be even having this conversation. "Come on, Corbin. Can't you see the truth of things? Our dates are cursed. It's best for us to just move on with our lives. Fake relationships are so high school anyway, I'm over it. Gray told you his secret, and he's doing well.

Wasn't that the whole reason you wanted me around? Well, guess what? We did what we set out to do, so now it's time for us to quit playing games and get back to our real lives. Let me be, Dr. Hottie, okay? I can't do this anymore, I just can't. I'm sorry. I want to, but... I just can't."

I had to steel myself against the unnatural brightness in Corbin's eyes. He started to say something then stopped. Instead he simply closed his mouth and walked away. After the elevator doors closed behind him, I slid to the floor, putting my back to the register as I pulled my knees to my chest and cried.

When Tracy found me a few minutes later, she squatted down in front of me and pulled me into her arms. "Oh, honey. What did you do?"

"I just broke up for real with my fake boyfriend and now I think I'm gonna die. Can someone die if their heart breaks in two? Because I'm pretty sure that's happening right now. Why did you leave me alone? I said things that I can't take back. I shouldn't be left unsupervised. Don't you know that?" When I sobbed harder, Tracy just hugged me through it. She left me a few times when customers came up, but other than that she was right there until I calmed down.

"Feeling a little steadier yet?" she asked when I was all cried out.

I shrugged listlessly. "I guess. My stomach feels like lead and I've lost all will to live, but that's just another day in the life of a diva, right?"

"Andy, don't take this the wrong way but I'm gonna need you to take your ass home. I can handle the cart by myself today. You're not going to be worth a damn today anyway. Go home and enjoy the rest of the day. You've got the whole weekend before you have to face Corbin again on Monday." She smiled kindly, but the look in her eyes told me that she meant business. *Damn stubborn-ass woman.*

I started to argue but then I remembered the pint of Chunky Monkey hidden in the back of the freezer at home. I held out a hand to Tracy so she could hoist me up. I whipped off my apron and slipped it under the counter. "Thank you, doll face. Just for this, I'll cancel all my well-laid plans for the glitter bomb I was going to hide in your car." Tracy just rolled her eyes and pointed resolutely toward the exit.

When I got home, I headed straight for the freezer to get my precious ice cream, and then it occurred to me how quiet the place was. It wasn't just because Gams wasn't around, I realized as it dawned on me that no evil minion had greeted me at the door. I didn't hear any slobbery snuffling at my feet, and nothing was growling at me. The silence was downright eerie. Closing the freezer, I started clicking my tongue against the roof of my mouth as I called for devil dog. "Where you at, Beelzebub? Here boy." I made kissing noises, as if that would ever induce him to come to the likes of me.

I walked through the whole house, but there was no sign of him. When I spotted the back door, my breath caught in my throat. The metal plate we slid into place at night was still blocking the doggie door, keeping him from getting inside via the rubber flap. Dammit, I'd been so out of it that I'd forgotten to take the night door off when I got up this morning. Now that I thought about it, I remembered having opened the door to let him out after breakfast. Shit. Why hadn't I remembered to remove what I secretly thought of as the dog-blocker at the same time?

Opening the door, I stepped out into the yard to call him again. Damn, it was too warm out here today for a dog of his breed to be stuck outside. With no real snout, his breathing issues didn't do well in the heat. I was getting worried when I didn't hear the familiar sound of tags jangling.

Jeebus didn't come when I called, but as I wandered around the yard, I heard a faint whine from around the side yard. When I walked around the corner, the poor baby was lying on his side in the barren remains of last summer's garden. I rushed over to him, only to find him whimpering and bleeding from his empty eye socket. It only took me a second to realize that he'd gouged out his only eye on the dried-out husk of a dead tomato plant.

Scooping him up in my arms, I blinked back tears as I cradled him against my chest. "I'm so sorry, Jeebus. I didn't mean to leave you out here all day. You have my permission to hate me from now until the end of time because this is my fault, baby boy. I forgot to clear out the garden and remove the dangers. And then I accidentally locked you outside and left you alone to suffer all day? I don't care if you call your satanic master and sic the beasts of hell on me, honey. I surely deserve it."

While I was talking in a soothing tone, I was quickly making my way back into the house to retrieve my keys before heading straight out to my car. With no other place to keep him, and unsure whether I should set him down, I drove one-handed all the way to the vet's office with Jeebus cradled against my chest.

The vet tech took one look at the poor little thing and rushed him back while I was left to wait and quietly panic. The tech came out to talk to me for a few minutes and let me know that Jeebus was recovering from surgery and waking up from his anesthesia. She gave me a pamphlet about living with a blind dog and a pat on the shoulder before disappearing into the back again.

I was sitting there looking at the brochure and blinking back tears, still freaking out about my day from hell, when I heard my name. "Andy?" I looked up to see Gray standing there in a dog groomer's smock.

My eyes bugged out to see him standing there. Of all the damn people in all the world... "Gray? What the heck are you doing here, honey? Shouldn't you be at school right now? I'm sorry, I don't know how to feel about seeing you here. This is weird."

Gray came over and sat down beside me, his eyes widening as he looked at the brochure in my hand. "Technically I am at school. Didn't my dad tell you about my community services class? This is where I volunteer. Becca and I both work here, isn't that cool? Even though it's volunteer, we're only allowed to work fifteen hours a week, but we get class credit. Becca says it will look good on our college applications in a couple years, but I just like doing it. But enough about me, why are you here?" He nodded toward the brochure. "Is everything okay with Beelzebub?"

My lip trembled as I shook my head. "I forgot to take the night door off when I left this morning and he was locked outside all day. He lost his eye on a dead tomato plant that I didn't get around to clearing away. He's blind now and it's all my f-fault." I stuttered over the last word as I broke into tears.

Gray wrapped his slim arms around me and held me tight while I cried. He excused himself after a few minutes to get some tissues and came back, pushing the Kleenex into my hand before hugging me again. I felt silly seeking comfort from a teenager, instead of being the one to provide it—especially when the teenager in question was the son of the wonderful man I'd just dumped. Thinking about that, I cried even harder.

I didn't realize it at first, but at some point Gray's slim

arms were replaced by a stronger pair. I vaguely recognized Corbin's voice as he murmured in my ear. I didn't know how or when Gray had reached out to him, but I didn't hate knowing that he'd come. "Let it out, babe. I'm here and it's going to be okay."

I sniffled against his shoulder as I began to ramble. "No it won't, how can it be? No matter what happens, I'm always going to be alone. Gams is going into that convalescent hospital, I just know it. I couldn't hold on to you, and I can't even take care of one little devil dog. I didn't really hate him, you know. I played it up, because that's just my style. What kind of an asshole would hate a dog? Now he's going to think forever that it's my fault he's blind. And it is my fault! All because I didn't clear out the garden, I literally made him get his eyes stabbed out. What's wrong with me?"

As I started sobbing all over again, Corbin made shushing noises. "You've got to quit taking responsibility for everything bad that happens, babe. It's going to be alright, and no, nobody is going to blame you. Accidents happen. Jeebus won't hate you. Don't you know that dogs aren't capable of hate? He plays that shit up just as much as you do. Now come on, Jeebus is ready to go home. Let's get out of here, what do you say? Will you let me take you home?"

I pulled back, wiping my eyes on the back of my arm before blowing my nose into a tissue with a loud honk. Corbin waited until I was done and then asked again if he could take me home when I didn't answer. I thought about that for a second and realized that I was in no place to drive right now. With a quick nod, I hesitantly agreed. "Yeah, that will probably be for the best. I can get my car later. But, Corbin? I want to go home to my own home, okay? I'm sorry, but I think I need to be alone."

That seems to be my fate anyway.

20

CORBIN

"That's it, Corbin. I'm sick of watching you mope around. Either you talk to him, or I will. It's been three weeks, and you two still haven't kissed and made up? I'm over this, you need to fix it. I don't believe a word he said to you that day. He was obviously talking from a place of fear, not from his heart." Dana reached for one of the dreaded pastries, breaking it in half and taking a bite. "For Pete's sake, he was having a damn pity party. You can't accept a breakup from him. He's too damn adorable. Get him back, dammit."

I smiled sadly as I set my coffee cup down. After I'd taken him and Jeebus home a few weeks ago, Andy had gone back to icing me out. Most days, he was nowhere near the coffee cart when I went for my morning coffee. All I got was an apologetically evasive Tracy and a cup of coffee that just didn't taste quite right anymore. But then again, nothing tasted right now that the sunshine had left my world. When I felt Dana staring at me, I held my hands out helplessly. "What can I do? He won't even serve my coffee anymore. I haven't laid eyes on him in over a week. He's always gone when I show up. And the girl he works with isn't telling me anything. Honestly, I'd be happy if he'd just let me talk to him as a friend, I'm worried about him. Loretta was moved a couple weeks ago to the convalescent hospital over on Sycamore, and I know that's got to be hard on him. I hate that he's all alone, but he won't let me in."

Dana waved her pastry at me while she chewed the bite that was in her mouth. "See? This is what happens when you go and get a case of real feels for a fake date. You guys didn't have any real commitment to keep him here, so it was easy for him to just slip away. Dammit. Now he needs you, and his own stubborn pride is probably keeping you apart. Well, that and the little fact that he didn't know that you gave a shit, if you ask me. I get that you're hurting. Hell, I am too. That boy is a doll and I was planning to make him my second bestie." She gave me a slow wink. "Only because I can't replace you completely; Becca might take issue with that because of Gray. But trust me, Andy was definitely going to be in the mix."

I rolled my eyes and propped my elbow on the table so I could rest my chin against my palm. "What can I do? Do you have any idea how empty my life is now that he is not in it? I had no idea how dreary my life was before him, and now that I've experienced the light that he brings, I can't go back to this shadowed half-life. I want my sunshine back, Dana. I want Andy."

Dana patted her chest, fluttering her eyelashes and happily sighing. "I swear to God, if this was a Disney movie we'd have had singing animals while you gave that speech. Why didn't you ever tell Andy all that? I feel like this past month could've gone so much differently if you'd just told him how you feel. Why can't people just communicate? Gah!"

"Did you miss the part where I said that I didn't know what I had until it was gone? How could I have told him when I didn't know it myself? All I know is that I need to find a way to make him see reason." I dropped my hand, lifting my head and staring at Dana in shock as a thought popped into my head. "Holy shit, I think I'm in love with him. Does it sound as crazy as I think it does when I say that? I mean, we haven't even had a successful date. How can I be in love with the guy? But then at the same time, why wouldn't I be? He's amazing. Shit, Dana. Our entire relationship was all fake, except maybe it wasn't? I don't know. Making it real wasn't in the original arrangement, but that's all I want now."

"You were faking it?" I looked up to see Gray and Becca standing in the doorway with matching looks of surprise on their faces.

"Dammit, this is what I get for talking to my best friend while you two are home. I'm sorry, Gray. I didn't mean for you to overhear that." I took a deep breath and decided to spill the beans. If I was going to be honest, I might as well get it all out there so that there weren't any more lies waiting to pop up at an inopportune moment. "Gray, I knew about you being enby before you told me. That's how I met Andy. Well... kinda. He's been serving me my morning coffee for the past year and a half, but we'd never really talked. I went to drag night at Saint's Place and we worked out a favor swap."

Gray didn't seem too upset. If anything he seemed more intrigued than anything else as he and Becca came to join us at the table. "Really? How did you know?"

Dana blushed and waved her hand. "Sorry. That's my bad; if we're going to do true confessions, I guess I'll play along. I kind of dug for information from Becca and told your dad. I had my suspicions when I saw the smeared eye makeup the day you came in to get your tooth fixed. But honey, we weren't trying to be nosy. It's just that you'd been getting into those fights and we were worried about you."

Gray thought about that for a moment, then shrugged. "I guess it's okay. Especially since that crap at Rockford High is over now, right? It's been a while and I'm happy at my new school. I'm just kinda bummed about Andy. At least now I know why he hasn't been texting me as much. He probably feels weird about it, if you guys aren't together. What happened? Did you guys fake break up or something?"

I shook my head. "I guess? Andy ended our fake

relationship after his grandmother got hurt. He felt guilty that we were out on a date when she fell."

"Wait, why were you on a date if your relationship was fake? See, that's the thing that doesn't add up and why I was surprised to hear that you were faking. Because you guys really fooled me. You were so good together. It was like you were friends and were also into each other. That was like hashtag lifegoals for me." Gray reached out to rest a hand on my shoulder, giving it a squeeze as he caught my gaze to let me know how serious he was. "I mean, for real, Dad. I don't think I've ever seen you as happy as you were with Andy. Maybe when Mom was alive? I don't even know. I was too little to remember much about that time."

Becca finally spoke up, the intrigued look on her face reminding me of the same exact expression that Dana always got when she was settling in for a good gossip. "So what was the whole deal about the favor that you guys swapped? You didn't tell us that part."

Dana turned to her daughter, her eyes dancing with delight. "They decided to trade a favor for a favor. Corbin wanted a fake boyfriend that would help him connect with Gray, while Andy needed someone he could pass off as a boyfriend to his grandmother so she wouldn't try to fix him up. You know how much he loves his grandmother, right? He'd do anything to make that lady happy, even if it took pretending to have a boyfriend. Isn't that just the sweetest?" Becca's eyes practically had hearts popping out of them and she and her mom gave matching dreamy-eyed sighs.

Gray grinned at the two of them and turned back to me, talking like one of those Valley girls in a classic eighties flick. "Like, that's totally awesome, Dad. That's just, like, the sweetest, you know? Like, oh my gawd. Can you even?"

For the first time in the month since Andy had originally decided to ghost me, I found myself laughing and feeling lighthearted for a split second as I laughed along with my son while the girls threw pastries at us. I flinched away from a highflying cheese Danish, turning back to Dana with a smirk when it landed with a sploosh against her wall before doing a slow, cheesy slide down to the floor. "And that, ladies, is why we don't throw food in the house."

I barely had a chance to register the narrowing of Dana's eyes before I got smacked in the face with a cherry Danish. Dana nodded smugly when the kids burst out in peals of laughter while I wiped the thick cherry glaze off my nose.

"I'm sorry to interrupt, Corb. I believe you were saying something about throwing food in the house?" She threw her head back with a quick laugh. "See, I don't mind making a mess if I'm prepared to clean it up." Holding her pointer finger out and making a wide circle toward my face, she smirked again. "Seeing that look on your face will make every minute of cleanup well worth the while."

Dana snickered while Becca held her phone up and took a picture of me.

Gray started bouncing in his seat. "Wait, chill out everyone. I figured it out. I know what Dad needs to do to get Andy back for us."

Grabbing a napkin, I attempted to wipe my face while I turned to Gray. "Back for *us*? What, do you think that we are all going to be in this relationship if I can get him?"

"Ew, gross." Gray scrunched his nose with distaste, holding his phone out as if he'd been about to show me something. "No. You can have all of... whatever your personal relationship would entail. When I said us, I meant that as in getting him back into our lives and making him part of our family."

As Becca and Dana nodded along, it occurred to me that we really had created our own little hodgepodge family here—and damned but if Andy wouldn't fit right in. With that in mind, I nodded toward his phone. "So what is it I need to do?"

Gray scooted his chair around so that he was shoulder to shoulder with me. "Okay, what you need to do is make a grand gesture. Hold on, I need to show you some of my favorite YouTube videos. This is going to be awesome."

21

ANDY

Late Tuesday afternoon, I was visiting the care home and frowning at the dust that was accumulating again on the houseplants I'd brought in to cheer up Gam-Gam's room and make it feel a little more like home. I mean, damn. Was there a log mill nearby that I was unaware of? Where did all this dust come from? I looked around until I saw the spray bottle I'd left in there to spritz them with and made short work of the task while my gams watched me with thinly veiled amusement.

Once I'd finished, she patted the bed next to her. "Over here, princess. I think it's time that you and me had a little talk."

I gasped dramatically as I dropped down to sit on the bed beside her, holding a hand to my heart as I shook my head. "No, Gams. Anything but *the talk*. I had to live through the hetero version from your son a lifetime ago, and my brain is still recovering—don't even get me started on the more pertinent parts of my body. Let's just say that if I ever need to make an inopportune erection disappear, all I have to do is remember that little conversation and voila, it disappears."

Gams gave a raspy chuckle. "All right, brat. That's enough of the comedy act. None of those distraction tricks from you today, got me? We're going to sit here and have us an important conversation."

I was afraid of where this was going, but I had to let her say the words. Holding one hand behind my back, I crossed my fingers and chanted inside my head. *Please don't tell me you want to go into a home. Please don't tell me you want to go into a home. Please don't tell me you want to go into a home.*

"Princess, I've decided it's time for me to go live in a retirement home." *Dammit. She said the words.* I opened my mouth to argue, but she held up a hand to stop me. "I want you to listen to me, kiddo. Just because we won't be sharing a house anymore, doesn't mean we aren't still family. You and me, we're way too tight for a little bit of distance to separate us. And it's not as if I'm moving to Japan, for God's sake. I'll only be living six piddly-ass blocks away. But I want you to hear me, so pay attention. I don't want any more half-ass caregivers coming in to help me live a half-assed life while you chain yourself to me."

"Gams, don't be silly. I don't chain myself to you. For one thing, you don't have enough hair on your chest for that kind of kinky action." I tried to joke, but Gams patted my hand, stopping me cold.

"I'm being serious right now, Andy. I don't like the shit I'm hearing where you have decided yet again to quit living your life because of me. How many boyfriends have you lost because you wouldn't spend the night with them out of some misplaced idea that I needed you home to keep an eye on me? How many dates have you turned down because there was something going on in my life? I don't want to see any more of that nonsense. It's time for you to get out there and live for yourself. I'm not going to be around forever, although I do plan to give the reaper a damn good fight when he tries to come for me. But when that day does come, I don't want you left all alone."

I flinched at the truth of her words, looking down at the bedspread rather than facing her just then. "That's not fair, Gams. As for my ex-boyfriends, I didn't lose anything when I kicked them to the curb. If they couldn't handle me being loyal to the one family member who'd given so much for me, then they weren't man enough for me in the first place. Trust me, I'm living my life. You should've seen me last Thursday down at Saint's. I'm here to tell you that Kandi slayed. I mean, she was on fire, girl."

Gams ran her hand up my arm, tugging at my shoulder to make me face her. "I'm glad you have your drag family, princess. But they won't keep your bed warm at night. Tell me something, honey. If you're living your life, then why aren't you seeing Corbin anymore?" When my eyes widened, she merely lifted a brow. "Come on, kiddo. Do you really think I don't have my spies reporting in while I'm stuck in this bed? I know everything that's going on in your life—and everything that isn't. You need to get your shit together and get your man back. Word on the street says that he misses you, and you can't tell me that you don't feel the same. Get over yourself and give him a call. Either that or quit hiding out when he comes to see you at work."

I huffed out a laugh and nodded. "Fine, the next time I see Corbin come in to my work, I won't avoid him. Does that satisfy you?"

Gams snorted. "Satisfy me? Girl, please. For me to be satisfied I'd need about a fifth of whiskey, a carton of Virginia Slims, and a handful of double-A batteries for BOB—my battery-operated boyfriend." Gams cracked up at the look of horror that must've crossed my face. "What? Did you think you're the only one in this family who can shock people? Listen, princess, you come by that shit naturally. It's embedded right there in our genetic code. Now, are you ready to let me tell you about the care home, or do you need a little more time to pout?"

When she reached up to pat my cheek, I leaned into her palm and closed my eyes for a second. "All right, old woman. Tell me about this hellhole you're planning to put yourself in when you've got a perfectly lovely home already waiting for you."

She chose to ignore that and blithely began to describe

where she planned to move. "First of all, it's not an old folks' home. It's a lovely senior care community. I'll have a small apartment of my own, with full-time nurses on staff. All of my meals will be catered if I can't make it to the dining commons, and they even have maids to come and clean up after my ass. There are activities and plenty of other old fogies for me to hang out with, instead of sitting on my ass at home. I'll be playing bingo, going to movie nights, hell, I can even do arts and crafts or take a damn yoga class if I want. They offer everything there. And more importantly, I'll have a better quality of life while you actually get to live yours."

I thought about that for a second and realized that I didn't hate the idea for her. Gams had become such a homebody after her bypass. It would be good for her to be out socializing again. "That sounds great, Gams. But can you afford it? Not to be nosy, but those places are pretty pricey and we're not exactly the Rockefellers."

Gams cackled, rubbing her hands together like an old movie villain. "Princess, you have no idea how much money I've got put away. I was saving it for my old age, but I might as well dig into it now. Not only can I afford it, but I'll rather enjoy spending the money that your father mistakenly thinks he's going to inherit. As for you? You're welcome to live in my house as long as you want, because it's going to be yours now anyway. But I don't want you to feel trapped, you hear me? If you get a better offer, such as one that might involve sharing a bed with a certain doctor, I hope you'll have the sense God gave a gnat and jump right on that shit. If and when the day comes that you don't need it, I figure you can use the house as a rental for extra income, or you can sell it."

When I started to argue that I didn't want her house, Gams smacked my arm with the back of her hand. "Hush, now. I've given this a lot of thought, and this is what I'm gonna do. I want to make sure you're taken care of just like you've always taken care of me. And since I don't want that son of mine fighting you when I'm gone, or you paying those stupid inheritance taxes, I'll be transferring the deed to your name before I move into the home. Oh, I almost forgot the best part. My sweet baby Jeebus can come with me and live there too. They encourage us to have dogs because of the comfort they offer."

For some reason, hearing that she was planning to take my little nemesis away was too much to bear. "Gams, now you've gone too far. You can't leave me and then turn around and take Beelzebub away too! Then I really *will* be all alone. Besides, he's still getting adjusted to being blind. He's used to our house and his yard. What if he gets out and is lost? Not to mention the fact that the new place will be scary and confusing for him."

"He'll be just fine," Gams said patiently. "I've already talked to his vet. All I need to do is give him some time to adapt. I'll have as many of his familiar things there as I can, which we'd want to do anyway. His food and water dishes, pillow and blanket—these things will give him comfort and help him settle in. As for you, baby boy, you've gone and gotten too settled in. I love you to death, so I'm going to say this as kindly as I can. It's high time for you to get out there and live your life out loud. Quit worrying about whether or not you'll get your heart broken. Not everyone is like my asshole son and the rest of your so-called family. Your trust issues have issues, but you really don't have to wait for the other shoe to drop every time you put yourself out there, princess. Take a risk and just be yourself with all your peacock glory. Be your colorful self, be loud and proud, and reach for that brass ring. You deserve it, honey."

My heart thudded against my ribcage as I looked at Gams in horror. "First you're telling me you want me to get back together with Corbin, and now you're trying to marry me off? I don't want to get married! I mean, maybe one day, but you know my rules. I have to date him for at least a year before I can even consider something like—"

Gams shut me up by putting her hand over my mouth. What was up with the women in my life always putting their hands over my mouth? *Sure hope they washed, because if not, that would just be nasty.* Gams waited until she had my attention. "I didn't say shit about a wedding ring, kid. And I'm pretty sure that would be a gold one anyway, maybe platinum? But definitely not brass. Reaching for the brass ring is a completely different thing. Which you damn well know. If you didn't have Dr. Pain in the Ass on your mind, you wouldn't have made that leap. Go on. Tell me I'm wrong, I dare you."

When she finally pulled her hand away, any snarky retorts

I'd planned withered away as I slumped my shoulders in defeat. "I don't know how to get him back, Gams. I was awful ugly to him. What should I do? Tell me."

Gams pulled me back so she could reach my cheek to give it a kiss. "You should get your ass out of here and go get your man, sugarplum. Stop making me repeat myself about living your life. Quit making a martyr out of yourself for me out of some misplaced sense of duty. I didn't rescue you when your asshat of a father kicked you out because I'm some saint or something. All I did was act like a decent human being who loved her grandson. Now I mean it. I want you to quit using me as an excuse to hide from life. Promise me, Andy."

Stretching out on the hospital bed beside her, I loosely wrapped my arm around her waist as I kissed her cheek and snuggled up beside her for a few more minutes. "I promise, old woman. I'm going to do my best to make you proud."

"Princess, you already do that just by waking up in the morning and being you. Keep on doing that, and you won't go wrong."

❖

I was watching the clock all day, thinking about the conversation I'd had with Gams the day before and waiting for my shift to end so I could call Corbin. I was going to see if I could talk him into trying a third date. Not that I'd blame him if he told me where to get off, after I'd frozen him out for a month like a spoiled diva.

When the lobby started filling with more and more people, and the line in front of our cart kept getting longer, I turned to Tracy in confusion. "Is there a convention in town and nobody told me? We've never had a crowd like this before. Remember that whole cursed date I told you about? Here we go again. I was planning to call Corbin after my shift and ask him out. Maybe see if I could get a second chance, you know? Well, maybe that's out because I'm pretty sure this is someone upstairs telling me that isn't in the cards for us. I mean, this is worse than the plagues of Egypt. When do we ever have a line this long, let alone at almost four o'clock in the afternoon?"

Tracy snorted and rolled her eyes. "Quit looking for excuses. Although I am glad to know that you're finally going to give that sweet man another chance. If I have to look into his puppy eyes one more time and tell him some lie about you being on the phone with the main office and too busy to make him a latte, I'm going to stab you in the eye with a fork." She gasped as if remembering Jeebus' accident. "No, my gawd. Forget I said that. Let's go with the gut. Yeah, that'll work. I'll stab you in the gut with a fork."

The nurse who was waiting for her coffee laughed at Tracy. "No, honey. Forget the gut, that would get too bloody. Besides, if you really want to make him pay, stab him in the sweetmeats. You know what I'm saying? Just shove that fork right smack into the family jewels, that'll teach a man who's boss."

I made the sign of the cross over my chest before grabbing a tray to block my crotch. I wagged a finger at the nurse. "I can't believe a medical professional would suggest such a heinous act. You're an evil woman, madam. Purely evil."

The nurse snickered, flashing me a wink. "Honey, you haven't begun to see evil. Catch me on my lunch hour sometime, I'll tell you all about some of the fantasies I've had on dismembering my ex-husband. Or I could tell you some war stories from the ER that will make your blood curdle."

As Tracy passed the woman her coffee, I looked past her to the line that was still growing. "It's a sea of scrubs up in here. Is every nurse and doctor in the building planning to get an afternoon coffee at the same time? Are we running a special and no one told me?" I turned to Tracy with a frown as a more pertinent thought hit my brain. "Shit. Do we even have enough stock on hand to serve all these people?"

Tracy nudged her chin toward the line. "I don't know, you might be surprised. Hey, I'm starting to see some familiar faces."

When I turned to look back at the line, the nurses who'd been at the front had stepped aside and Gray had taken their place. Becca and Dana were standing beside him with... Mama Honey? My jaw dropped open when I saw that Larry was in full Honey Combover regalia on a weekday afternoon. My breath caught in my throat as I leaned over the counter to make sure that we weren't about to have a snake infestation up in here.

I breathed a sigh of relief when I found that Honey wasn't risking getting arrested for indecent exposure. She was wearing zebra print spandex leggings instead of a short skirt. Not that shiny spandex was much of a step up, especially with the lewd bulge that was prominently on display beneath the gauzy, un-belted tunic she wore over her red velvet corset. When I noticed that Mama Honey had one large hand resting on each of the kids' shoulders, I figured the apocalypse was drawing nigh. It had to be if my two worlds were combining like a handful of mixed berries in a blender.

Gray grinned as if he'd read my mind. "Hey, Andy. I hope you don't mind that Miss Honey is hanging out with us today. Larry is our glee director at the new school. Did you know that he's also friends with Becca's uncle Nick?"

Honey tossed her hair over her shoulder. "Mama Honey just had to come say hello when the kiddos here told me they knew you. I had no idea my sweet little Grayson was Dr. Hottie's son. He's the star of my glee club this semester, just wait until you see him go at the Spring Choral." She paused to lift an elegant brow, scrunching her nose with a frown as she took in my workday uniform. "Oh, gurl. We have *got* to get you a job with a better uniform. Either that or a rich husband."

I rolled my eyes at Honey and turned to ask Gray or Dana what I could get for them. Before I could ask their order, all four of them opened their mouths and broke into song. My jaw fell open as they sang the first line of one of my favorite Queen songs.

Can anybody find me...

It took me a moment to realize that the entire lobby was humming the harmony line. Honey and the others stepped to the side and the crowd parted like Moses at the Red Sea as a beautiful tenor voice picked up the next line of the song.

Each morning I get up I die a little...

My eyes about bugged out of my head when I saw that Corbin was the one singing while boldly walking toward the counter with hands held out in supplication. He sang loud and proud, serenading me the entire way.

This was actually happening. In the damn lobby. At work. On a Wednesday!

Tracy was squealing, holding her phone up with one hand to record it all while her other was wrapped around my waist. She somehow managed to jump up and down while whisper-shouting in my ear. *"Holy shit, he's giving you a flash mob moment!"*

The two sides of the lobby where the people had separated for Corbin began doing a perfectly choreographed routine, snapping their fingers and dancing in the background while Corbin paused halfway to the counter and continued to sing. There was so much happening, I didn't know where to look whenever I managed to tear my eyes off my boo.

When he sang the line *I ain't gonna face no defeat*, I almost swooned. My cheeks began to ache so much, I reached up to see if I was being bitten by a pair of twin Godzilla spiders or something. I was surprised to realize they hurt because I was smiling so hard. My face was probably gonna get stuck like this—not that I cared if it did. It would be the perfect souvenir of the most epic moment this town had ever seen.

As the crowd began chanting the chorus line—*find me somebody to love*—I realized that a huge-ass bouquet of roses was being passed through the crowd, each person taking it then twirling and bending with a flourish as they passed it along. The bouquet reached the counter just before Corbin. It ended up in Gray's hands and as he passed it to me, the entire room went silent as he sang the final line—with a twist.

"Won't you please give my dad somebody to love?"

I started to take the bouquet, looking for Corbin until I realized that he'd disappeared, never having made it to the counter. Tracy gently nudged my shoulder, turning me to look beside the cart. Corbin was standing there, holding his arms out wide.

That was all the invitation I needed. I took off at a run,

jumping up into his arms. His smile was as wide as mine felt as he lifted me up, holding me up over his head and slowly spinning around in a circle like we were starring in *Dirty Dancing* and I was playing Baby to his Johnny. I felt like we were literally in the freaking movie as he slowly lowered me for a kiss. By the time our kiss ended, my arms were wrapped around his neck and my legs around his waist. I was clinging to him like a horny koala as he began to carry me away while everybody clapped and cheered.

Tapping his shoulder to stop him, I looked back toward the cart. "Wait, boo. I don't want to forget my roses."

Gray was grinning from ear to ear as he jumped up and down, waving the bouquet over his head. "Don't worry, Andy! I'll keep your roses safe, you get out of here and go have a big romantic moment with my dad that I don't ever want to hear about."

Everyone applauded while my prince carried me away.

22

ANDY

By mutual agreement, we ended up back at my place. Jeebus was overjoyed when he scented Corbin walking through the door. I kicked my shoes off, tugging at Corbin's hand to get him to follow me while he bent to greet the devil dog. "Come on, boo. I promise the little stinker will be here when you come out. But first you need to come back to my room so I can show you my etchings."

Corbin chuckled as he stood, wrapping his arm around my waist and pulling me against his chest for a kiss. "Funny, I was hoping I'd get to see your *etchings* at some point."

I slipped out of his arms after a quick kiss, pulling at his hand as I backed toward the hallway. "The magic happens down here, preferably behind a closed door with Jeebus on the other side. He may be blind, but I'd still feel like he was watching us."

Jeebus ran between Corbin's legs, bumping into his left foot and nearly tripping my poor boo in his frenzy to snarl and bark at me. "Whoa, you need to slow your roll, Beelzebub. Growl all you want, but this man is mine, bitch," I laughingly scolded the dog as I danced out of his reach.

Corbin scooped the evil fuzzball up to snuggle him against his chest, scratching Jeebus under his chin as he crooned into his ears. "Be a good boy, Jeebus. I promise I will give you a turn later for belly rubs, but right now it's Andy's time." He followed me down the hall while he soothed the savage beast. If he'd been a cat, Jeebus would've been purring at this point.

"I swear, if you think you're bringing that dog into my bedroom, then I hate to tell you, but you've got another think coming," I said over my shoulder, glaring jealously at the malicious canine who was stealing away Corbin's attention with his satanic charms.

When we reached my bedroom, Corbin paused in the doorway and turned to set Jeebus down. "Sorry, boy. It's the end of the line for you, buddy. Remember what I said, be a good boy." He held his arm out in the direction of the living room and snapped his fingers. "Go on, go lie down." Jeebus cocked his head to the side, looking all pitiful and cute as he whimpered in the back of his throat. Corbin simply snapped his fingers a second time, speaking in an authoritative tone. "You heard me, go lie down."

My jaw dropped when Beelzebub happily obeyed,

running off with his tail wagging. Grabbing hold of his arm, I yanked Corbin into my room and closed the door behind us. "While I'm shocked by what I just saw, on the other hand I totally get it. If you ever snap your fingers and use that daddy tone on me, I'll probably wag my tail and rush to obey too."

Corbin chuckled as he grabbed me by the hips, pulling me snugly against him. "Oh, yeah? You liked that, did you?" I shivered as he breathed into my ear, the beard he'd grown during our time apart tickling the sensitive skin on my neck in all the best ways.

My hands moved to tug at the hem of his shirt, sliding it up so I could get to his skin. "Nghh, that beard though, boo. So hawt... I don't know what made you grow it, but I gotta tell you, I'm already a fan."

While he was busy kissing along my neck and jawline, I was doing my best to feel him up and finally memorize the curves and dips of his muscles. My hands stilled when he stopped to look at me with sad eyes. "I don't know if I should tell you why I grew it. I've been thinking of it as my breakup beard. I was just going through the motions when we were apart and after that first couple of weeks, I realized I'd gotten pretty scruffy. I went to shave, but ended up just grooming it instead when I decided that I kinda liked how it looks."

I closed my eyes for a moment to let that sink in. I'd given this man enough pain that he'd gone for two weeks without shaving? I opened my eyes when I felt his hand cup my face, seeing Corbin shaking his head with a gentle smile. "We have plenty of time to talk about all that later. But before we go any further, I want you to know that I don't blame you for the way things went down this past month."

Huffing out a breath, I ducked out of his arms and walked over to my bed. I sat down on the side and braced my hands on my knees as I looked up at him. "I guess I killed our big moment, didn't I? Me and my big mouth, I just had to flap my yap when the two of us could've already been dancing naked instead." I winced as I thought about how badly I'd behaved when I'd ghosted this man. "I'm sorry I shut you out and dropped you flat. That wasn't right. I was afraid of getting my heart broken, so I guess I thought it would be easier if I were the one who nipped things in the bud."

Corbin squatted in front of me, taking my hands in his as he gazed into my eyes. "Babe, can we just agree to move on with no recriminations? I'd say that I forgive you, but I can't do that because there's nothing to forgive. Yes, you hurt me when you shut me out. The relationship may have been fake, but our connection and friendship weren't. My life was empty without you in it, but see, I never would've known that if you hadn't done a runner. I was just drifting along, happy to let things happen naturally. I hadn't given any thought to my feelings until there was nothing left to think about but my raw emotions."

I leaned forward to press a soft kiss to the corner of his

mouth. "I missed you too. So much. And for the record, I didn't know what I had in you either until you weren't around. There were so many times over these past weeks when I wanted to shoot you a text or call you to tell you something funny that happened, but I couldn't. And since it was my fault because I'd chosen to book a one-way ticket to the pity party of the century, not a minute went by that I wasn't kicking myself in the ass for being so damn stupid."

"No, babe. Don't say that. You weren't stupid, you were coming from a place of fear and self-preservation. I get that. And why wouldn't you have? I didn't give you any reason to think there was a chance of us getting serious. Let's just promise each other that in the future, we'll communicate our worries instead of bottling them up or letting them keep us apart. I'm just glad today went well; I was halfway afraid you'd think that I was a stalker instead of enjoying the grand gesture."

My mouth fell open. "Shut the front door! Are you freaking kidding me? That was the most epic moment of my life. I'm pretty sure that Tracy recorded it, and I hope that hussy knows I'll need a copy because I can't wait to see it again. But you should probably know something. Gams had a long talk with me yesterday, I mean, my girl took me to church with the sermon she fed me. But after our visit, I'd already decided to call you when I got off work today. I was going to ask you out again. I figured we could see if maybe the third time was the charm."

Corbin's smile nearly took my breath away. "Really? That would've made my day. But I'm glad I made yours first. You deserved a big romantic moment. And I needed to give it to you, if we're going to start things off right this time around. With that in mind, I had my own idea for our third date. And if you say yes, I'll be spiriting you away this evening. But more about that later. Right now, I think we both have way too many clothes on." He glanced toward my nightstand and back at me. "I'm embarrassed to admit this, but I didn't exactly plan ahead. Please tell me that you have supplies."

"Honey, please. A diva is always prepared." I pulled my hands from his and jerked my shirt over my head, tossing it over my shoulder.

"I think you are confusing a diva with a Boy Scout." Corbin winked as he stood and started to casually undress like it was no big deal and we'd done this before.

"Really? Tell that to some of the leaders I had as a kid. Honey, you haven't seen a drama queen until you catch a couple of leaders on the third day of a five-day campout and the s'mores supplies run low." Following his lead, I was undressing while we talked.

"Why do I feel like that's coming from personal experience?" Corbin stood there, stark naked with a hand slowly stroking his cock.

I nearly swallowed my tongue as I watched. After a few

seconds, I couldn't remember what we'd been talking about. "I'm sorry, did you ask me a question?"

Corbin rushed forward, scooping me up to throw me on the bed. "Nope. Conversation time is over."

"Thank fuck because I think we have much better things we could be doing with our—" Before I could finish my sentence, Corbin stretched over me, pinning me beneath the weight of his body as his lips covered mine. I was right, there were much better things we could do with our mouths.

Where I was ready to rush things along, thrusting my hips to rub our erections together, Corbin was on a different page. "What's your hurry, babe?" He pulled my roaming hands off his back and moved them up to the headboard. "I'm in charge this time, okay? Can I trust you to keep them here, or will I need to restrain you?"

My dick jerked at the sound of that. "Ooh, if you want to tie me up and have your way with me, I won't argue, boo."

Corbin chuckled against my ear, the vibrations sending a fresh round of shivers down my spine as he rolled off and got onto his knees beside me. "Maybe we'll save the bondage for next time. Flip over on your stomach for me, babe."

Never one to argue with a good suggestion, I rolled right over and wiggled my butt with a silent invitation. Which reminded me... "The supplies are right there in the nightstand, help yourself."

Reaching over me, he did as I suggested, dropping the lube and a condom beside me on the bed before turning his attentions back to me. Straddling my hips, he knelt on all fours as he bent to kiss the back of my neck before moving downward. Every inch or two, he'd pause to rub his beard against my skin, marking me like a cat before kissing the flesh and moving on to the next spot. He slowly moved backward on the bed, kissing and marking me as he went. Before I'd realized what was happening, he was stretched out between my legs, his hands spreading my cheeks apart while he rubbed the sides of his beard over my balls and taint and up along my crack, then back down again.

"Sugar Honey Iced Tea, you're trying to slowly kill me here." I moaned into my pillow when I felt the moist tongue lapping over my rim. His hands nudged my hips forward while the beard rubbed against my balls as he worshipped my hole with every millimeter of that wicked tongue.

My hand snuck down without my consent, easing under my belly to wrap itself around my cock. I only managed to get a few strokes in before I felt a rush of cool air against my ass. I felt the bed shift and looked back over my shoulder in confusion to see what had happened to my new best friend, Mr. Tongue. I watched while Corbin rummaged through the top drawer of my dresser. "You need something, boo? Surely it could've waited, no?"

Corbin turned around with a triumphant smile as he held

up one of my belts. "Roll back over, babe. I told you to keep those hands over your head, didn't I?"

Oh, snap. My cock twitched at the look on his face. I licked my lips and slowly rolled over, lifting my hands over my head to grip the rail on the headboard. As Corbin straddled my shoulders to fasten my hands in place, I lifted my head and strained to get a taste of the heavy cock that was bouncing just out of my reach.

Once he was done, Corbin tugged on the belt to test his handiwork, smiling down at me with satisfaction. "Let's try this again, shall we?" His heavy cock bounced again as he moved back. I whimpered, still straining to reach my elusive treat. Corbin's eyes filled with heat, his pupils so dilated that the gray in his eyes was merely a silvery outline around those dark pupils. Grasping his cock, he slapped it against first one cheek, then the other. "Was my babe trying to get a taste of this?" I nodded quickly, licking my lips as I stared at the leaky tip. "All you had to do was ask, babe."

I groaned as he slowly fed the tip into my open mouth. I tried to lick and tease the head, but he kept pushing forward. All I could do was let my jaw go slack and take a deep breath before he shoved it farther inside. Bracing his hands on either side of my head, Corbin slowly rocked his hips, his eyes never leaving mine as he fucked my mouth. He wasn't so big that I couldn't take him all the way, but I still choked and gagged each time he went a little deeper. He went all the way in, holding my head flush to his groin until I had to lift my knee to bump his butt when my eyes started to bulge out and I felt a little faint for a second.

Corbin immediately pulled out, his eyes filled with concern. "Take a breath, babe. Was that too much?" He dropped the boss vibe for a moment, looking suddenly unsure of himself. "I didn't hurt you, did I?"

I gave my head a quick shake, dipping my chin toward his cock. "Hell, no. You will only hurt me if you stop. Give it back, I just needed to get some air. I'm good."

"If you're sure, but just grunt or kick me again if you need a break. That worked well." This time he went a little slower, treating me so gently that he was making me regret my need to breathe. I wanted to close my eyes and get lost in the moment, but at the same time, I didn't want to look away from his gaze. I went to grab his ass, my hands jerking against the headboard when I forgot that I was restrained for a second. Corbin pulled his cock out of my mouth, laughing as he moved back. "I'm going to have to buy some handcuffs or something, babe. I think I like having you at my mercy."

"Just remember one little thing, boo." I fluttered my lashes as I told him the same thing I always said to Tracy. "Payback's a bitch, and so am I. Don't be surprised if you wake up someday to find yourself spread-eagle and handcuffed to the bed posts. Not because I'm minding this, don't get me wrong. But I can't help but think that I should give you a taste of being the one getting spoiled when you're at my mercy."

Corbin moved down my body again, this time rubbing his beard and kissing along my chest. The way he kept mixing things up between the slow and sensual and back to the rough and bossy was hot as hell. "Fuck, yesss..." I moaned as he rubbed his beard against my balls while slowly licking up my shaft. Taking my length into his mouth, he returned the favor as he slowly bobbed his head, sucking with just the right amount of pressure to keep me on the edge.

I didn't see or feel him grab the lube like a freaking ninja, so when I felt a slick finger push into my hole, I rolled my head from side to side as nonsensical babble spilled from my lips. *"Fuckity fucking fuckballs. Fuck a duck. Fuck a buck. Fuck a truck. Fuck a... a...* shit. What else rhymes with fuck that still makes sense?"

When he chuckled around my cock, I saw fucking stars. He added a second finger, pumping them in and out of my rim with the same rhythm as his head while he bobbed up and down. I closed my eyes, biting into my lip. I'd never enjoyed being prepped this much in my life.

Fuck me sideways, I was right there. I felt the familiar buildup of liquid heat shooting to my balls and groaned again. "Mhmm. I'm gonna have to give you a few hours to quit doing that, boo." I bit my lip as I moaned, pumping my hips to make him take me deeper. Corbin simply chuckled again, this time pulling away and leaving my cock with one final kiss to the tip—the evil, edging bastard.

Before I could get a single snarky word out, Corbin was

stretched over me, his lips pressed against mine while he slowly pushed his tip through my entrance. I sucked in a breath, moaning at the delicious burn as he filled me. One arm slid beneath me, lifting and cupping my ass in his palm while the other slipped under my head, holding me in place as he deepened our kiss. Our tongues slid together while his hips began to move a little faster.

I felt like I was melting into the mattress, pinned under his weight and loving every second. Releasing my head, Corbin broke our kiss and let me drop against the pillow as he slid his hand down my body to cup both ass cheeks, lifting my hips as he sat up on his knees and began pounding into me a little harder. In this position, he was able to get deeper than he had before so that Darth-Vader-helmet-shaped head of his cock rubbed against my prostate with every thrust.

"If I'd thought it through a little better, I would have restrained you differently so that I could flip you over." I blinked at the sound of Corbin's voice, so cum-dumb that it took a second to realize what he was talking about.

Flashing him a slow wink, I rasped in a low, sultry voice I barely recognized, "That's okay, we can save it for next time. I'm just about..." I bared my teeth, jerking forward, my tethered wrists straining against the headboard as I thrashed. "Nghhh... I'm... holy fuuuuck!" My dick came, untouched, shooting strands of thick, milky cum onto my abs.

"Holy shit, your ass is clamping around me with an iron

grip." Corbin threw his head back, grunting as he lost his rhythm, his hips taking on a mind of their own as he came. After his cock stopped pulsing, Corbin dropped his head forward, looking down at me as he sucked in several hard-fought breaths. "Damn, I know it's been a while, but I don't ever remember coming that hard."

"I know you're not trying to talk about past experiences while your dick is still lodged in my ass, right?" I grinned up at him as I teased. I probably could have come up with something better, but I was too well-fucked to be witty right now.

Corbin winced as he gripped the base of his cock and slowly pulled out. Rolling off the condom I had zero memory of him putting on in the first place, he tied it in a knot and staggered off the bed in search of... something. Once I had more than two brain cells firing, I realized what he wanted. "There's a wastebasket by my desk, and wet wipes on the dresser that will work for cleanup, if you don't mind." He came back over with a couple wipes and cleaned the cum off me before undoing the belt. While he went to throw away the wipes, I rolled onto my side and rubbed my wrists.

The bed dipped as Corbin curled up behind me like a big spoon and wrapped his arm around my waist. "I didn't get that too tight, did I? Your wrists look red."

I glanced back over my shoulder, pursing my lips for a kiss. After he obliged me with a gentle kiss, I pulled back and held up my wrist so he could see it better. "No, I'm

HOW NOT TO BLEND

perfectly fine. My skin just marks easy, it's the curse of being a blond. Although..." I paused to waggle my eyebrows for effect. "Since I'm easily marked and have a high pain threshold, that does lead to interesting possibilities for the future. Just sayin'."

Corbin dropped his head against my back, his shoulders shaking with laughter. "The sweat and cum haven't dried from our first time and you're already planning to pull out the whips and chains, huh?"

"Hey, you started it." Now that the blood was returning to my big head, I remembered something he'd said earlier. "So, you were saying something before about a date?"

His head popped up with a broad grin. "Yes, I can't believe I almost forgot. We need to get going if you're on board because I took the liberty of making us reservations."

I flipped around in his arms, needing to be face-to-face for this conversation. "Reservations? I'm intrigued —keep going."

Corbin blushed as a hesitant look flashed through his eyes. "You can still say no, but Tracy said if you're on board, she can call one of the weekend people to cover your shifts tomorrow and Friday. And Dana will keep Jeebus for you, Gray's staying over there anyway."

Blinking rapidly, I tried to make connections between what he said but nothing was making sense. "Sorry, boo. You're gonna need to elaborate. What am I supposed to get on board with, because you kinda skipped a major part of your invitation there."

"Oh! Sorry." Yep, there went that blush again. He looked so adorably chagrined that I couldn't do anything other than kiss him. After I pulled away, he stared at me for a moment as if trying to remember what we'd been talking about again. "Oh, our date. Right. So, this isn't anything fancy, but I thought maybe it would be good for us to run away for a few days."

I stared back at him for a moment, my brain going haywire. "Honey, I am *not* eloping on the first good date. Also, you should probably know that I have a rule about marriage—we'll have to date for a minimum of one year and four complete seasons before any vows or rings are exchanged."

Corbin grinned, pausing to kiss me before he spoke. "As much as I don't hate that idea, believe it or not, that's not what I'm asking you. There's a cute little bed-and-breakfast a couple towns over. Nobody will know where we are, and we can have privacy to work on our relationship. I took the next two days off, like I said, and Tracy said she could arrange the same for you. I figure if we leave tonight, that gives us three nights if we come back on Sunday."

I dropped a quick kiss on his cheek before wriggling out of his arms and jumping off the bed. Corbin sat up, watching me as I ran around the room, yanking doors and drawers open and gathering clothes. "What are you doing, babe? You never answered my question."

Pausing with an arm full of clothes, I looked over at him and thought about that for half a second. "I didn't? Huh. Well, you can go ahead and consider me your plus one, given the fact that I'm trying to pack. Now why don't you be a good partner and grab my suitcase off that high shelf in the top of the closet?"

He grinned as he stood and stretched before walking over to the closet to do as I'd asked. "Huh. If I'd known getting you to go out of town with me would be this easy, maybe I'd have invited you sooner."

"Please, boo. You know you had me at four days away. As long as that includes you and me getting horizontal so much that we both come back walking bowlegged, I'm good with it." I grinned at the sound of Corbin's groan.

I didn't miss the fact that his cock was already back at half-mast as he dropped the suitcase at my feet. "Did you say both of us will be walking bowlegged? Because I'm totally down with that."

"Oh, honey. It's adorable that you'd even think you wouldn't be getting beneath me at some point this weekend."

23

ANDY

The five of us went out to dinner on Sunday night after Corbin and I got back to town. Jeebus had been ecstatic to have Corbin return, but all I'd gotten was a growl when we left again, almost immediately, to treat Dana and the kids to dinner.

Gray kept looking back and forth between me and his dad with a big old grin. When he saw me catch him, he didn't bother to pretend, instead motioning between the two of us as he spoke. "So now that you guys are together, does that mean you'll be moving in with us at some point?"

Dana's eyes danced while Corbin looked horrified. I simply waved my fork as I shook my head. "Whoa, sugar. Let's not put the cart before the horse. Daddy doesn't get to own the pig just because he got a little sausage, no offense. A girl needs to be wooed, boo-boo. Besides, Gams is giving me her house. I really need to figure out my own shit before I can move forward, you know?"

"Okay, but will you come spend the night sometimes?" I wondered what was up with this kid's obsession with me sleeping under the same roof.

Before I could ask, Corbin held up his phone. "As much as I hate to leave this rather scintillating conversation, my service is trying to get a hold of me. I'm going to step outside; you guys go ahead and eat without me."

After he left, Gray shrugged unapologetically. "I'm not trying to put you on the spot, Andy. I'm just trying to figure out what comes next."

Now that, I understood. "What comes next is your dad and I date and see where things go, while you and I continue being friends. We're still bros, boo-boo. We still texted when I wasn't seeing your dad last month, didn't we?"

Gray shook his head. "Maybe, but nothing like we did before. You acted weird. It was like you felt bad talking to me. I guess I just need you to promise that if you guys break up again, you won't break up with me too."

Fuck me, this kid was breaking my heart. "I'm sorry, Gray. I didn't handle that right, with either of you. I really don't want to go into this relationship planning to break up, but I can offer my promise that if it does happen, I won't let it affect our friendship again."

"Cool, that's all I wanted." Gray nodded like it was no big deal then scooted his chair back and stood, dropping his napkin onto his chair. "Excuse me, I'll be right back."

I watched as he headed for the alcove at the back of the room where the bathrooms were located before I went back to my meal. While I fed my face, Dana and Becca filled me in on everything that I'd been missing. While Dana showed me a video on her phone that someone had sent her of the big flash mob, Becca interrupted, grabbing her mom's arm and making the phone fall to the floor.

"Careful, baby. I'm still under contract with this model," Dana said as she bent to scoop the phone up. "If it breaks right now, I'm still going to be paying for the dead phone for another year."

Becca looked so anxious, she was practically vibrating in her seat. "I'm sorry, Mom. It's just that I'm starting to think that Gray has been gone too long, and look who's sitting over there."

Dana and I followed Becca's line of sight and my stomach did a flip-flop when I saw Harold Danvers and a mousy-looking woman sitting across the room. There was a third place setting at their table, but whoever had been sitting there was absent. I whipped my head back to Becca, my heart thumping with alarm. "They're out for a family meal, aren't they? That means that Clark is here somewhere."

At her nod, I got up and rushed to the men's room without further comment, my spidey senses fully activated. When I opened the door, I walked in to find the bullying mofo holding Gray against the wall, his forearm against Gray's throat as he snarled into his face. Before I did another thing, I pulled my phone out and hit the emergency button that would connect me with police dispatch. As soon as someone answered on the other end, I whispered that I needed help in the men's room at Cattlemen's then put it on speaker as I walked farther into the room so they could hear what was happening.

"I told you you'd be dead meat if you told anybody that I'm the one who beat you up. What did you do, Lacy Gracie? You talked and then I had cops at my door. I'm letting that go since nobody believed your ass. But you'd better be on guard, you little fag. You'd better not be telling people anything to make me sound gay. People are talking about how your dad's walking around with a fucking fairy; I don't need that shit in my life. If you tell anyone that I almost let you kiss me, that last beating I gave you will look like a love-tap."

I'd heard enough. "That's right, his dad *is* walking around with a fucking fairy—special emphasis on the fucking, because that's the best part." I held up my phone when Clark looked over his shoulder to see who'd interrupted his moment of torment. His eyes bugged out as he realized that we were on speaker with the police station, and the kid released his hold on Gray as he spun my way. I caught Gray's eye and tilted my head toward the door. "Get out of here, boo-boo. I've got this, you go get your dad." Gray nodded and took off while I tucked my phone in my pocket and braced myself for whatever the little shit thought he was going to do.

When Baby Huey took a step in my direction, I channeled my inner Britney and turned with a swift cheerleader sidekick straight to the balls, bringing him to his knees. While he was down, I rushed out of the bathroom, pulling the door shut behind me. There was a straight-backed wooden chair sitting just outside the door, so I grabbed it and wedged it under the knob, knowing it wouldn't hold long but might just keep him there until the cops could arrive. I sat down on the chair, hoping to help keep him from escaping.

The doorknob rattled as he fought to open it. My heart was racing as I sat there with a white-knuckled grip, trying to ignore the pounding and muffled curses coming from the other side of the door. When I heard a splintering sound, I jumped off the chair just in time to avoid landing on my ass when he finally managed to jerk it open. Right as he came bursting through the doorway with a furious look on his face, a pair of cops came through the dining room with Corbin and Andy right behind them.

The cops were putting him in cuffs, already reading off his rights when Harold came over, his face purple with rage. "What do you think you're doing, officers? This is unlawful arrest. You unhand my son this instant, don't you know that he's a minor?"

One of the officers held up a hand. "Sir, your son is being arrested, minor or not. For a listing of his charges, you will need to meet us downtown. Feel free to call an attorney, but there's nothing that can be done right now. These gentlemen are pressing charges, just as I'm sure the restaurant will when they see the property damage that's been done to their door." While Harold continued to scream bloody murder, Corbin came around and pulled me into his arms. Gray was on the other side of me, hugging me and resting his head against my shoulder while I slid an arm around his waist.

As the cops started to walk Clark away, I called out after him. "Your life doesn't have to be this way, baby bear. Forget about your father's homophobic bullshit. If you ever want advice about how to pick up a boy the right way, let me know. I'll be happy to teach you how to do it without forcing yourself on them."

Harold spun around, jabbing a finger right in my face as he snarled. "You shut your filthy, fagotty mouth. My son is nothing like you and that little queer kid you're protecting. You and all the other members of your rainbow posse can just shove your gay agenda up your ass because you're never going to get a chance to turn him into one of you."

Corbin knocked Harold's finger away from my face, cocking his fist back and socking him right in the nose. "You don't get to talk to my boyfriend like that, Danvers. You keep your own filthy mouth shut, you hear me?"

Harold fell right on his ass, blood pouring from his nose as he screamed at the officer who'd stood there witnessing the entire display. "Arrest this man, I'm pressing my own assault charges. You're my witness, you saw what he did."

The officer shook his head with a comically confused look on his face. "I'm sorry, Mr. Danvers. I have no idea what you're talking about. I didn't see a thing, except for that part where you just verbally abused these gentlemen with your hate speech. Is that what you're talking about? Because I can hardly arrest the victim, now can I?"

A vein bulged in Harold's forehead as he struggled to push his way up from the floor. After he was on his feet, he shoved past us with a malevolent glare as he rushed off to see to his son. I shook my head as we watched him. "Now that's a man who needs to meet Jeebus, *bless his heart*."

I looked up at Corbin and tipped my head toward Gray. "Whatcha say we get them to box up the rest of our meal and go back to your place? I don't know about you, but I kinda need a change of scenery after seeing the kind of riffraff they serve here."

24

CORBIN

I winced as Andy treated my abraded knuckles. "Calm your tits, boo. I'm almost done and then we can ice it." Andy's no-nonsense chiding had everybody laughing at my expense. Gray was way too amused, if you asked me.

"Damn. I forgot how bad it hurts to punch someone." I rolled my shoulder after Andy released my hand, surprised to even feel the tension all the way up there. He was back a moment later, wrapping an ice pack over my knuckles.

Gray snickered. "That's why we use our words, remember, Dad? What is it you always say? Gentlemen use their words; only Neanderthals speak with their fists."

"He's not wrong, I have heard you say that on multiple occasions." Dana wasn't helping, and I shot her a playful glare to let her know just that. Honestly, I really didn't care if I had been a hypocrite by using my fist. I'd punch that fucker again any day of the week and twice on Sunday, if it came to it. Nobody got to threaten my man or my family, let alone use filthy words like he had and poke his finger in my man's face.

Jeebus stood next to the chair, snuffling around my feet and trying to figure out what was wrong. Poor baby, he couldn't see me, but he knew that something wasn't right. Andy groaned with an exaggerated eye roll when Jeebus stood on his hind legs and tried to climb onto my lap.

"Hey, babe. Would you lift him up here for me? I can't with my hand wrapped in ice. The poor little guy is worried about me." I tried batting my lashes at Andy the way he always did, but it didn't have the same effect since everyone at the table started laughing and mocking me. They sat there blinking at each other like a bunch of owls with an eye infection. "Stop it." I laughed. "That can't be how I looked when I tried to bat my lashes."

Andy snickered. "You're right, it was way funnier the way you did it." He stooped to pick up the dog, gently setting him on my lap. Jeebus growled when Andy scratched under his chin. "Did you see that? I keep telling y'all this dog is demonic. I feed him, I show his nasty ass affection, and what does he do? He tries to bite me or he growls at me—and that's when he's not trying to knock me into a puddle of piss." Andy sat down and leaned back in the chair, looking around the table at everyone. "Beelzebub aside, this is nice, right? Being here together and laughing, despite everything that went down back at the restaurant. Do you think it will always be like this?"

Before I could answer, Dana looked up from her phone. "I sure as hell hope so. This family is past due for happiness. Now that we have our own drag queen in the mix, it's bound to be a lot more fun up in here."

"That reminds me." Andy's face lit up as he turned to Dana. "You're going to have to tell me what you thought about Honey. But first, before I forget—I want you to come with Corbin and see my show this week. The kids are old enough to stay home, right?"

Becca and Gray both rolled their eyes and shot Andy matching looks of what I liked to call resting teen face, where they'd look at a person like he or she were the biggest fool that had ever walked the earth. Andy didn't play though. "What? You'd better not be looking at me with those *duh* expressions, kiddos. I'll tell Mama Honey on your asses."

Dana and I both cracked up as the kids rushed to apologize. Becca was halfway through an explanation of how she'd been thinking about something else and her expressions must have been misleading when Dana shook her head and turned back to Andy. "Yes, I'll be there this Thursday. I wouldn't miss it for the world, especially after the reports I've heard of snake sightings at those shows."

Instead of sitting at the bar and talking to Nick like I normally would, tonight I was seated at a small table near the stage so that Dana could have the full experience. When Kandi came on stage, the rest of the room fell away. I was entranced with every sway of her hips and the way she worked the room like a seasoned pro.

Tonight she was dressed like Britney from the single "I'm a Slave 4 U." The green belly dancer style bikini and colorful beaded ropes around her waist were hot as hell. But it was the pale-yellow rubber boa that sealed the look, even more than the see-through jewel-toned train that hung from her waist.

Dana was screaming at the top of her lungs while I pretty much swallowed my tongue when Kandi took the boa and flung it between her legs, holding it from front to back while she gyrated over it and lip-synched with the lyrics *Get it get it, get it get it*.

"Holy shit, no wonder you love these shows," Dana said during a quick moment between songs. "Kandi is dynamite. Or however you're supposed to say it."

"What you trying to say, darlin', is that my gurl slays." We both looked up when we heard Honey's deep, gravelly voice.

I pointed at the empty chair beside Dana. "Why don't you join us, Honey?"

"Oooh, I never turn down an offer from a gentleman,"

Honey said in a low purr as she sat down. Dana raised her eyebrows, biting her lip and obviously trying not to giggle when she noticed Honey's manspread as she leaned back with her long legs splayed wide open at the knee. Honey turned her attention away from the stage, looking at the two of us for a moment. "I don't normally talk about my day job when I'm here, but I'll make an exception. As you know, our school is connected to the Presbyterian Church. Make sure you don't miss the kids' performance on Sunday. We're giving the parishioners a taste of what they can expect this year during the Spring Chorale. I don't know if the kids told you, but they both have solos."

I shook my head, already pulling out my phone to make a note. "When I do go to church, that's where we attend. The church is why I was even aware of your school in the first place. But no, Gray didn't mention a thing about a solo this Sunday."

Dana looked just as irritated as I felt. "Neither did Becca's ass, so thank you for telling us, Honey."

Honey waved a hand. "It's my pleasure. Don't be hard on those kiddos, now. The two of them are shy about singing in front of an audience still. They're new, and you have to keep that in mind. We'll get them there, but it's gonna take time. At any rate, we'll see you on Sunday. Or I suppose I should say that Larry will see you on Sunday. Mama Honey doesn't do church, *okay?*"

Our conversation ended abruptly when Kandi switched

into her next number, one I hadn't seen her perform before. This time she was lip-synching the ballad "I Will Still Love You," and it was no less mesmerizing than anything else I'd seen her do. As she slowly walked down from the stage and strutted in our direction, the house lights went down and a lone spotlight followed along with her. There was a loud intake of breath that echoed around the room followed by the expected awwws as she came over to straddle my lap.

I rested my hands lightly on her thighs as my beautiful seductress leaned back as if to sing into her microphone. My breath caught in my throat when she leaned forward to gaze into my eyes as she mouthed the words to the lines *I finally know how love feels, Tell me if it's real.*

I was only partially aware of Mama Honey dabbing at her eyes while Kandi poured her heart out to me in song like we were the only two people in the room. I noticed Dana holding her phone up, undoubtedly recording the whole thing, but I couldn't be bothered to take my eyes away from my enchantress.

At the end of her song, Kandi set the microphone on the table and wrapped her boa around my neck, pulling me forward to first kiss my cheek and mark me with her brand before giving me a soft kiss on the mouth. After she pulled away, Kandi whispered in my ear. "Tell me it's real, Corbin. This is me—every part of me—telling you that I love you in the most public way possible."

Sliding my arms up to wrap around her waist, I hugged her

closer and whispered back, grateful for the loud music that afforded us this little bubble of privacy. "It's definitely real. And I love you too—every part of me loves every part of you, no matter what name you're using or what clothes you're wearing."

25

ANDY

"Ugh. Remind me again why I let you talk me into this?" I jerked the knot out of my tie and started the whole process all over again. "Really, don't you know that Sundays are supposed to be brunch days?"

"Hold still, I'm a pro with these." Corbin batted my hands away and took over the job of getting my tie properly knotted. The way he had his lips pinched together with the tip of his tongue poking out the side while he concentrated was too cute for words. He gave my tie a jerk as he tightened it, then used it to pull me in to steal a kiss. "Sorry, babe. If you want to cross the bridge, you gotta pay the toll."

"Isn't that what the trolls in the fairy tale told Billy Goat Gruff before they tried to eat him?" I licked my lips and took a step closer. "I mean, I'm not against you trying to eat me right now, if you want. But..." I shook my head with a sad smile, as if my heart were breaking. "You're the one that's dead set on going to church."

Corbin's laugh washed over me, making me feel warm and safe. "It's just church, I promise nobody's going to try and baptize you. The Presbyterians don't do anything crazy and you can set your clock by their service. I swear on all that's holy, you can put a damn pot roast in the oven on your way out the door and get home before the timer goes off—that's how well organized the services are here. I promise that our presbytery is all-inclusive, and even better? Our pastor is openly bi."

I walked over to sit down at the foot of the bed so I could put my shoes on. "Your pastor may be one of us, but doesn't the Danvers family attend there too? And isn't he like a deacon or something? I'm sorry, boo, but that doesn't exactly fill me with the warm and fuzzies for your church."

"He's a ruling elder, unfortunately. But keep in mind, he was elected into that position by the congregation. A lot of the people who put him there have either died or moved along due to age or the natural progression of things. I don't see him holding his position the next time around. We have too many newer, younger members that aren't as likely to put someone like him in power. And you have to remember, what we witnessed at the restaurant? He doesn't normally let people see that side of him. Butter wouldn't melt in his mouth when he's out and about with his public face on. He saves the homophobic slurs for behind closed doors or when there aren't any witnesses."

"You know what? I don't think his son is the real bully here, I think Danvers is the bully. And that poor kid is wedged so far in the closet that it's going to take years of therapy when he finally gets pulled out into the light of day." I held up a hand when Corbin narrowed his eyes. "Take a breath, boo. I'm not saying that what he did was in any way excusable. Gray is the one I care about first and foremost—I'm just saying that I hope somebody is watching out for the Danvers kid. If Harold acts as shady at home as he does around us, I shudder to imagine what he might do or say to his own kid."

Corbin came over and sat down beside me, biting his lip as he stared down at the floor, deep in thought. He finally looked up and leaned over to kiss my cheek. "You have a kind heart, babe. While I wouldn't cross the street right now to piss on that kid if he were on fire, I'll be the first one to sound the alarm if we find out that he's being abused. I don't care who you are or what you've done, nobody deserves that. Maybe the things that he's been doing were taught to him at home; it wouldn't surprise me."

As I listened to him talk, something settled in my stomach and I felt lighter than I had in years. "You know what? I'm happy that you're making me go to church with you today. You're the kind of Christian that I wish my parents had been. The fact that you'd be willing to stick your neck out for a kid who behaved so atrociously to your own says everything about your character and who you are. If that's what your version of Christianity is, maybe I don't have to hate it quite as much as I thought I did. You have to understand, the family that was supposed to love me yet so easily turned their backs on me and pretended I no longer existed were doing so under the guise of being good Christians. That's why the whole church thing is such a sticking point for me. But a part of me misses the community and tradition of being part of a church family."

Wrapping his arm around my shoulder, Corbin pulled me sideways into a hug. "Thank you for giving it a chance. To me, I don't care what your label is, who you vote for, or what church you attend—or don't attend. I care whether or not you're an asshole. I go to church because that's how my parents brought me up and I'm comfortable in the one I attend. But honestly? You can be Catholic, Protestant, Buddhist, Taoist, Wiccan or atheist or whatever the hell you want to be, and I won't judge or disrespect you. I only ask that people do the same for me. And as for making you go? I'm pretty sure that you're the one who insisted that you weren't going to miss your boo-boo's first public appearance. So don't be pinning that shit on me, babe."

I sniffed indignantly. "I know what I said, but I was still suckered. I was told that there was going to be a solo, not where said solo was taking place." When Corbin started to look concerned, the laugh I was holding in escaped. "Chill out, boo. If I'm being honest, I'm kind of looking forward to going to your church. I can't wait to see the look on Harold Danvers' face when we walk in there and he has to pretend that he doesn't hate us and everything we stand for. In fact, I'm almost inspired to become a regular member."

Gray popped around the corner of the doorway, poking his head in to check on us. "Are you guys ready? I can't be late and we should've left five minutes ago. I already fed the dog and left water out for him. So can we go?"

I stood and reached for my sports coat, slipping it on over my dress shirt and tie. After one final look in the mirror, I reached for Corbin's hand. "Come on, Papa Bear. Time to go watch our little boo-boo sing his heart out."

Gray looked relieved, chattering as we headed for the car. "Did Dad tell you to wear a suit, Andy? Because you would've been fine in a regular polo and slacks or something like that. Heck, some people even wear jeans."

I pressed the back of my hand to my forehead, groaning as if I were mortally wounded. "You're breaking my heart, boo-boo. You've obviously never been to the South. Going to church is the reason people own clothes called their Sunday best. What's the point in even going if you're not going to look your best and make everyone else wish they were as fine as you?"

"Gee, Andy. I must've missed that portion of Scripture that mentions looking finer than thy neighbor." Gray grinned as he got into the back seat. We joked all the way to the church, and even though I knew that I'd be facing Danvers on the other end, I still felt much lighter at heart than I'd have expected as I walked into the one place that I'd vowed never to enter again in my life.

The service was surprisingly not awful. I wasn't expecting a fire and brimstone sermon, given that the pastor was bisexual and the church inclusive, but I still hadn't expected to feel quite as comfortable as I did. I smiled like a proud daddy, holding up my phone and recording both Becca's and Gray's solos, as well as the other songs done by the school's glee club. The highlight for me was seeing Larry in a sports coat and khakis as he led the singing. It always cracked me up when I saw his combover. Even though Honey's name was pronounced *come* over, it was a total play on his real-life combover. I wondered privately how many people in this congregation, not to mention the parents from the school, had seen their mild-mannered music teacher when Honey came out to play.

After church, Corbin and I walked out hand in hand, and while I noticed a few people giving us the side eye, the other parishioners were welcoming for the most part. We'd just stepped out onto the portico, nobody else within earshot, when Harold walked up to us.

His mustache went halfway up his nose as he sneered at our joined hands. "You two have a lot of nerve coming into the house of God after the filthy things you said to my son and the lies you told about him."

Before I could respond, the church's pastor walked up. He was about the same age as Corbin, and not hard on the eyes, even if he was a man of the cloth. "Harold, you need to keep your personal life at home and legal affairs away from the church, you know that. If the police arrested young Clark, they certainly didn't do it based on any lies. There was evidence, as well as the sworn testimony of the 911 operator who overheard his express confession. Come on, friend, you know that as well as I do. God is a God of love and we welcome all here at Grace Chapel. If you can't support that, perhaps it's time you resigned."

Harold gave the pastor a coolly assessing look. "You have a lot of nerve, Pastor Samson. Those are strong things to say to a ruling elder in front of parishioners. Don't think this won't come up at the next board meeting."

Pastor Samson stood his ground. "There are a lot of things that need to come up within the next board meeting, Harold. Perhaps we should sit down together and make a list, don't you think?"

Harold spun on his heel, walking away without further comment. The pastor held a welcoming hand out to me. "We haven't met, but please allow me to apologize for Harold. Trust me when I say that he's a dinosaur whose time has come and gone. If you stick around, you'll find that most of our church don't behave or believe in the same manner. But enough about him. He doesn't deserve any more free rent in our heads, as my father used to say. I want to thank you for coming today and for putting a smile on Corbin's face. I haven't seen this guy look this happy in, well... ever. But then, I've only known him for the past year since I was put in this position."

I smiled warmly as I shook his hand. "It's okay, Pastor. Harold doesn't bother me. He's just upset because his precious son got busted in the act of hurting our Gray and had to face responsibility for it."

Pastor Samson smiled sadly. "Young Clark is a tragedy waiting to happen. As you probably know, he was given probation and will be doing community service." Corbin and I nodded, but when a sneaky smile spread over his face, I knew the pastor was about to tell us something we didn't know. "After I spoke to the judge on his behalf, I suggested enrolling young Clark in a diversity acceptance and anti-bullying course, as well as anger management classes that we offer here at the church. I can't tell you any more than that, but I assure you that young Clark will be getting the help he needs, or so we hope, anyway."

I was still smiling at his words when Gray and Becca walked out of the church. As I looked over my boo-boo's fabulous outfit, it occurred to me that I hadn't paid enough attention before we left the house. Although he was wearing a standard pair of gray dress slacks like the rest of the glee club, his white shirt had a lace collar and pearl buttons. Now that his hair was nearly touching his shoulders, it was obvious that he'd taken a flat iron to it and added some product to make it shiny. He didn't wear a lot of makeup, but what he had on brought out his natural beauty. My favorite part of his whole ensemble was the confidence that shone out of his eyes now that he was happy in his own skin.

Becca was dressed in a matching outfit, and I was about ready to tear up at how damn cute they were. When Dana joined us, she was chattering about some in-home candle party she'd agreed to have, and I was only listening with half an ear until I realized that she was telling me that I had to come and buy something to help her out. My head whipped around to stare at her like she had two heads.

"Girl. Seriously? I had to leave the South just to get away from all the damn Tupperware parties. I don't care if it's candles, plastic ware, or marital aids—they're all the same. And they all want to make you one of their drones." I shivered dramatically, huddling against Corbin as if seeking the warmth of his protection while he and the pastor chuckled at my antics.

Dana just rolled her eyes and pressed on. "Sorry, honeybun. Not buying it, since you left there at eighteen. Nice excuse though, I'd almost have bought it if I didn't know your backstory. But you should know that as my new official second bestie, you have duties to perform, one of which involves coming to any and all in-home parties and making orders. Just be glad I'm not asking you to host a party." She looked around to make sure nobody besides our family was listening even though she lowered her voice to a stage whisper as she waggled her eyebrows. "The candles are paraffin, by the way. They burn at a lower temperature so you can use them in other places—hubba hubba."

"Ew, Mom. No! So much of the no." Becca groaned

260

miserably while Corbin and I laughed. Gray just took a step to the side as if to disassociate himself from us.

Pastor Samson smiled and excused himself to go greet more parishioners while we turned to make our way to our cars. I slipped my arm through Dana's and heaved a heavy sigh as if I were martyring myself for her cause. "Fiiine, you've convinced me to come to your damn party. But next time? Lead with the body wax, baby girl. You could've saved the whole spiel with that little nugget of info."

26

CORBIN

Andy swung our arms to and fro as we walked hand in hand through the downtown area. "I can't believe that it's already been six months and two whole seasons that we've spent together, boo."

I squeezed his fingers, bringing his hand to my mouth for a kiss on the next upswing before dropping it to let our arms swing again. The fact that he felt like he needed to fully experience four seasons in a new relationship was just another thing that I adored about him.

Glancing over at the relaxed smile on his face, I pulled him toward the bench where we'd stopped on our first date. "Let's take a break, babe."

As we settled down on the bench, we repeated our positioning from that first aborted date as he snuggled against me while I put my arm around his shoulders. Running my hand down the back of his arm, I bent to kiss the top of his head. "You're sure in a good mood, aren't you?"

Andy turned to peer up at me, puckering his lips in invitation. He didn't answer me until after he got his kiss. "What's not to be happy about? Gams and Jeebus are doing well in their new apartment. My hair is on point. We're on a date, and unlike that first one, neither of our phones rang or buzzed at the restaurant while we actually enjoyed an entire meal. Everybody in our family seems to have gotten the memo that they're no longer allowed to have emergencies on date nights, so yeah... I'm in a good mood."

I bent to kiss him again while I fumbled in my pocket. When I broke the kiss, I shoved a small velvet box into his hands. Andy stared at it for a long moment before looking back up at me. "I love you to the moon and back, boo. But this had better not be what I think it is." He pouted playfully, despite the trembling in his hand as he held the box.

I tucked the trembling hand into the back of my mind—a good sign that any future velvet boxes wouldn't be entirely unwelcome, provided all four seasons had passed. Nodding my chin toward the box, I rolled my eyes. "Hush, Andy. Just open the box, babe. I know damn well that my sweet little Kanderson-Anderson isn't the type of diva who gets married in the first year. Lord knows I've heard you on the subject enough times, haven't I? I wouldn't dare put you in such a position."

"Damn straight." Andy snickered. "Besides, there are way more interesting positions that we could find ourselves in, such as..." His voice trailed off as if he were thinking about positions. I poked him in the side where he was the most ticklish, making him giggle again. "Fine, I'm opening it!"

He sat up a little straighter and took a deep breath as if to fortify himself, then slowly opened the box. When he spotted the brass key lying against the black velvet, he sucked in a breath and looked up at me in confusion. "I thought you weren't pushing me? Is this meant to be the next-best thing? What, do you think since you're already getting the milk, now you're gonna get the cow for free? That is why you're asking me to move in with you, right?"

His eyes narrowed as I started to laugh. It took me several minutes to calm down enough to talk. I was still wiping tears away with the back of my hand as I stared into his indignant eyes. "Sorry, I don't know why that was so funny —but it really was. Babe, you're not an ingenue from the fifties who some wolf is trying to take advantage of, you're a grown-ass man, so the cow thing doesn't track. And for the record? I far preferred the pig and sausage metaphor to the cow and milk anyway, because I have a penchant for your sausage." As he visibly bristled as if preparing to unload a bucketful of snark, I leaned in and stole a kiss.

When I pulled away, I booped the end of his nose as he laughed. "You know what I love most about you? Your sassiness. But, no—this is not meant to be the next-best thing. This is simply me and Gray telling you that our door is open whenever you want it to be. Nobody is rushing you or trying to avoid buying livestock. But when you're ready to use the key on a daily basis, you'll have it. In the meantime, just use it to come and go whenever you want. Emphasis on the *come*." I couldn't resist adding that last part with a leer.

Andy thought about that for a moment, then surprised me by getting up to straddle my lap. He wrapped his arms around my neck and kissed me, obviously giving less than a fuck about what anybody walking by might think—yet another thing I loved about this man. When he pulled back, his eyes were filled with affection. "So here's my question. What if I decided to use it on a daily basis now? Would that confuse Gray, or have you not thought that far ahead?"

Clasping my hands around his waist, I briefly touched my forehead to his before leaning back with a smile. "Babe, the fact that you'd even think of asking that question says everything I need to know about whether or not I'm making the right decision. But I think maybe you missed the part where I said the key was from both me *and* Gray. He and I had a discussion and we've decided that we want you there with us, however and whenever we can have you. I love you, Andy. And I love Kandi. Like I told you all those months ago, I love every part of you. I want you in my life, in my home, and most importantly, I want you in my family."

Andy laughed almost nervously as he swiped a tear away

with the back of his hand. His eyes were still welling with tears as he nodded. "Yes. Okay. I'll do it. You had me at you and Gray deciding that you both want me, but you sealed it with the whole 'I love you.' I know we've said those words before, but the thing is that I really love you too and I don't want to be apart from you anymore either. I hate to say goodnight and head to a bed that you're not lying in with me. I want to be right in the same places where you want me to be—your life, your home, and more than anything in the world, I want to be in your family."

We sealed it with a soft, tender kiss, then Andy started bouncing on my lap. I grinned as I looked at my Peter Pan of a boyfriend whose large inner child was only exceeded by the size of his heart. "So, what should we do first?"

Andy gave me one more kiss before hopping up and impatiently holding out a hand for me to get up and move my ass. "That's easy. Now we go home and have hot sex to seal the deal about blending our lives, and after that we talk closet space while we bask in the afterglow of super-sweaty sex."

"Now that sounds like a plan; the trick will be to see how fast we can get there. Here's a thought, how about the first one naked when we get there gets to top?" I laughed at the totally fake scandalized look on his face and scooped him up, tossing him over my shoulder and swatting his butt as I ran for the car while he squealed with glee.

Yeah. Blending Andy into our family was going to be a lot of fun, and I was going to love every second.

When you have a crush on your dad's best friend and there's nothing left to lose but your pride, you learn... How Not To Wait

Get your FREE copy of How Not To Wait
https://dl.bookfunnel.com/mx2r9719ru

Twitter:
https://twitter.com/SusanHawkeBooks

Facebook:
https://www.facebook.com/AuthorSusanHawke/

THANK YOU FOR READING!

As an avid reader and big romance fan myself, I love sharing the stories of the different people who live in my imagination. My stories are filled with humor, a few tears, and the underlying message to not give up hope, even in the darkest of times, because life can change on a dime when you least expect it. This theme comes from a lifetime of lessons learned on my own hard journey through the pains of poverty, the loss of more loved ones than I'd care to count, and the struggles of living through chronic illnesses. Life can be hard, but it can also be good! Through it all I've found that love, laughter, and family can make all the difference, and that's what I try to bring to every tale I tell.

I'm a happily married mom with one snarky teenage boy, and three grown "kids of my heart." I'm more widely known for my mpreg writings as Susi Hawke; this new name is a departure from that. Whether written by Susan or Susi, the books are filled with that all-important love, laughter, and family I mentioned; the only difference is that this name has no male pregnancy. I look forward to sharing my stories with you, and to bringing more romance and laughter into this world that needs it so very badly.

facebook.com/AuthorSusanHawke

twitter.com/SusanHawkeBooks

Made in the USA
San Bernardino, CA
24 January 2019